Fresh and beguiling, the Bachelor Girls are an engaging new addition to the mystery scene. They tackle criminals with a combination of unique moxie and an irrepressible sense of adventure. I want to be friends with the Bachelor Girls!

Deanna Raybourn,
New York Times bestselling author of the Lady Julia Grey Mysteries

With the witty wordplay and inventive plot twists of a classic Sherlock Holmes mystery, McMillan spins a detective tale sure to delight and fascinate those who love entertaining novels full of clues and sleuths and lively characters that live long after the story ends.

Virginia Smith,
author of the Tales from the Goose Creek B&B

In her fabulous debut, Rachel McMillan brings 1910 Toronto to rich and wonderful life. The intrepid Jem and Merinda make a winning detective team. Full of romance and derring-do, *The Bachelor Girl's Guide to Murder* will keep you turning pages.

Nancy Herriman,
author of *No Comfort for the Lost*

Smart, sassy, and chic. *The Bachelor Girl's Guide to Murder* is all that and more. A fabulous historical. Encore, Rachel McMillan!

Laura Frantz,
author of *The Mistress of Tall Acre*

A wonderful romp! McMillan's delightful debut introduces us to a beguiling and intrepid crime-solving duo. The two lovely ladies defy expectations and social norms as they lead us across early twentieth-century Toronto and into the heart of a compelling mystery...with a dash of romance on the side. Can't wait for more of these two and the adventure they'll lead us on next!

Katherine Reay,
author of *The Bronte Plot*

A savvy and street-smart read. Rachel McMillan's *The Bachelor Girl's Guide to Murder* is a wickedly clever debut, with the wit and intelligence of a classic Agatha Christie whodunit. It's a vintage-inspired ride with a dash of mystery, romance, and just enough suspense to keep the reader guessing. I was drawn in and held captive with the turn of each page!

Kristy Cambron,
author of *The Ringmaster's Wife* and the Hidden Masterpiece series

One does not merely read *The Bachelor Girl's Guide to Murder*. Rather, one enters the story, allows the author to take her on a wild ride through early twentieth century Toronto, and remains unable to do anything but turn the pages until the final scene has ended. McMillan has created characters whose exploits will live on well beyond this story. Well done! Now hurry and write the next one!

Kathleen Y'Barbo,
bestselling author of *Firefly Summer* and *Sadie's Secret*

In her stunning debut, Rachel McMillan achieves a perfect balance of wit and warmth and invites readers into an entirely new world. More than intrepid detectives, Bachelor Girls Jem and Merinda are fully fleshed women, grappling with mysteries of the heart as well as those of the gritty streets of historic Toronto. A cast of supporting characters brings life and dimension, as well as the promise of more stories to come. McMillan's homage to the spirit of Sherlock and Watson stands solid on its own, whether in pick heels or brogans.

Allison Pittman,
author of *On Shifting Sand*

Come for the gorgeous cover and promise of mystery; stay for the lilting romance and tingling wit. Rachel McMillan's debut is the perfect mix of engaging characters and a fresh, enticing voice. Simply put, I'm hooked!

Melissa Tagg,
author of *From the Start* and *Like Never Before*

There's nothing more delicious than discovering an author whose novel is as fabulous as the cover art suggests. Debut author Rachel McMillan is a refreshing new talent in the inspirational market, penning an enchanting tale of murder, mayhem, and Sherlockesque shenanigans. Jem and Merinda will captivate readers' hearts as their adventurous spirits cause them to buck social norms for ladies of their day, resulting in humorous and dangerous consequences in equal measure. Toss in a charming Italian journalist with a penchant for verse and a dedicated member of the Canadian constabulary with a weakness for a certain woman, and sparks...and bullets...are bound to fly. Unique, witty, and invigorating, McMillan's prose is smooth, her historical detail excellent, and her bachelor girls appealing in every way. Sherlock Holmes and Phryne Fisher may need to step aside as Herringford & Watts, Lady Detectives, are on the case!

Rel Mollet,
Relz Reviewz

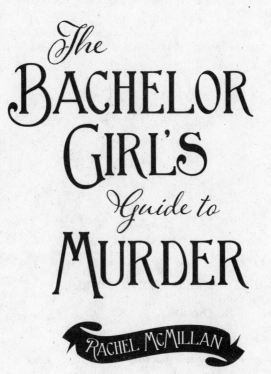

The BACHELOR GIRL'S Guide to MURDER

RACHEL McMILLAN

HARVEST HOUSE PUBLISHERS
EUGENE, OREGON

Cover by Harvest House Publishers

Cover illustrations © Snusmumr, sibiranna / Shutterstock

Published in association with William K. Jensen Literary Agency, 119 Bampton Court, Eugene, Oregon 97404.

THE BACHELOR GIRL'S GUIDE TO MURDER
Copyright © 2016 Rachel McMillan
Published by Harvest House Publishers
Eugene, Oregon 97402
www.harvesthousepublishers.com

Library of Congress Cataloging-in-Publication Data
    McMillan, Rachel, 1981-
    The bachelor girl's guide to murder / Rachel McMillan.
        pages cm — (Herringford and Watts mysteries ; book 1)
    ISBN 978-0-7369-6640-5 (pbk.)
    ISBN 978-0-7369-6641-2 (eBook)
    1. Women detectives—Canada—Fiction. 2. Murder—Investigation—Fiction. I. Title.
PR9199.4.M4555B33 2016
813'.6—dc23

2015028830

Printed in the United States of America

16 17 18 19 20 21 22 23 24 / BP-JC / 10 9 8 7 6 5 4 3 2 1

FOR
MAISIE

Acknowledgments

Thanks go to...

My Tante Annette, who gave me not only my first copies of *A Room of One's Own* and *Jane Eyre,* but a lifetime of a strong female role model to look up to.

My agent, Ruth Samsel, who called and said, "What about a female Sherlock Holmes?" and who always believed in my girls as much as I do.

Allison Pittman: You are the wind beneath my wings. I couldn't have done any of this without you. #TeamMcPitt

Kathleen Kerr, who has not only proven to be the brains behind this entire operation but also a truly kindred spirit.

My sister, Leah Polonenko, for the Easter Sunday at St. James that got me over the finish line.

Jared and Tobin, for popping the champagne and celebrating every milestone thus far in my writing journey.

Jessica Barnes, Jessica Davies, Sonja Spaetzel, Team Shiloh, Joanne Bischof, William Murdoch, Martha Kroeker, Bernice Wong, Chelsea Jarman, Christina Jolly, Tim Jolly, Rick and Barb Turnbull, Gina Dalfonzo, Ruth Anderson, Lori Smith, Melanie Fishbane—I love you all.

Gerald and Kathleen McMillan, who always believed that this bookish, anxious, hyper-romantic writer girl could do anything she put her mind to...especially if she kept Matthew 6:33 close at hand.

JEMIMA,

Your father and I have decided that, after giving you several opportunities to prove you are pursuing a proper course for a lady of your station and background, we can no longer financially support your endeavors.

While we applaud your dedication to your job at Spenser's, we think it is high time you settled down. Your father and I have long tired of presenting you with eligible suitors, only to have you dismiss them to follow Merinda Herringford around like a bee to honey. We have long felt, and expressed, that she is not fit company for a lady of your potential.*

As we seem to be making no headway in securing you a future worthy of your breeding, we can only keep you in our prayers and hope that soon you will see the error of your ways, return to your upbringing, and recognize that a lady of your not inconsiderable age (honestly, Jemima, four-and-twenty is hardly the age to be gallivanting about Toronto unwed) should be making prudent strides toward securing a husband.

Please see the enclosed pamphlet suggesting appropriate activities for young ladies who are, as you should be, in pursuit of a proper husband...

---

* The word *potential* was always used liberally by Jemima's teachers at the Susanna Moodie School for Promising Young Ladies.

To the Ladies of St. James Parish

Hone your domestic skills, enjoy the company of other young Christian women, and even increase your potential of meeting your future husband.

Sunday: After-service box social

Tuesday: Sewing Circle for the benefit of the heathen children of India. Bring your needles and thread.

Wednesday: Visiting the invalids and shut-ins

Thursday: Crokinole

Saturday: Harvest Dance. Please see Hyacinth for raffle tickets.

Chapter One

A proper lady's activities of choice are as important as the embellishment of her sleeve or the turn of her head. A potential suitor will want to see which hobbies and interests pique the attention of a lady before he pursues her. Ensure your selection boasts fine company, creative accomplishment and, in relevant cases, healthy and wholesome competition.

Dorothea Fairfax's Handbook to Bachelor Girlhood

Toronto, September 1910

A murder scene is no place for a proper lady."

Merinda Herringford tilted her chin defiantly and stared at Constable Jasper Forth with an icy eye. "Then it's a good thing I'm not a proper lady."

Merinda had just declared, rather crassly, that it was "about time for a good murder." And Jasper, powerless under the stare of her bright cat eyes, had had little say in the matter. She'd trailed so closely behind him as he'd set toward the Elgin Theatre that she'd scuffed the polished heels of his shoes.

Jem Watts swatted the constable playfully on the shoulder. "Yes, Jasper, it's a good thing she's no proper lady."

"I'd get in hot water if they knew I brought the two of you down here." He swallowed. "What was I thinking?"

"You were thinking it's about time the police sought out someone as clever as me. And a woman to boot!" Merinda lifted her skirt, which was already an inch or two higher than respectability and fashion allowed, and stepped to the opposite side of the corpse. "She was strangled."

"The rope burns would indicate strangulation, yes."

"But there was no struggle. Look at her arms. Free of bruises."

The constable had doubtless reached the same conclusion, but he grinned as he watched Merinda. "You're a smart egg." He narrowed his eyes. "For a woman."

Jem peered at the corpse more closely as Merinda flashed a glower at Jasper. She was surprised that the body failed to inspire more horror. The white contours of the young woman's face, the flames of her bright red hair, the freckles sprinkling her nose and cheeks, the mouth drawn wide, round, and unsuspectingly calm...Why, she might have been sleeping, though her translucent skin and the blue-green veins in her upturned arms said differently.

"I wonder who would do such a horrid thing," Jem said, muffling her voice with a raised handkerchief. "She can't be more than seventeen."

"There's no smell of decay yet, Jem." Merinda spoke without moving her gaze from the body. "You can put your kerchief away."

"Maybe they're her smelling salts," said Jasper gently.

"I don't need smelling salts!" protested Jem.

"What was she doing here, anyway?" Merinda swooped down. "She's not dressed the part."

The girl's homespun dress, apron, and rubber-soled boots were out of place in the foyer of the grand theatre where she had been discovered. True, her red-gold hair seemed a fit for the luminous interior of the theatre, but the rest of her was oddly mismatched.

"Name's Fiona Byrne. She was from Corktown," Jasper supplied, "in the employ of Tertius Montague, a member of his house staff."

"Really?" said Merinda.

"When Jones and I first got here, Montague was identifying the body."

Merinda's eyes widened. Tertius Montague, mayor of Toronto,

was known to be a benevolent mogul. His thumbprint brushed half a dozen philanthropic enterprises, from hospitals to affordable housing in St. John's Ward, the poorest part of the city. A regular King Midas. Recently, he had decided to invest in the cultural expansion of Toronto, and the Elgin Theatre—a modern and beautiful space like those in New York and Chicago—was his latest addition.

But he was most familiar to Jem and Merinda as the creator of the Morality Squad, a band of plainclothes detectives who rumbled through the city arresting women suspected of incorrigibility or vagrancy. Lately, an offense as slight as a short hem or loitering after dark* could merit an arrest.

Montague was using his Morality Squad as a weapon against the immigrant women of Toronto—it was his trump card to move up in the polls for his reelection campaign. He vowed to return the city to "Toronto the Good" of the previous century. Montague was neck-and-neck in the polls with the reformer Horace Milbrook, but he had the backing—and the deep pockets—of Thaddeus Spenser, owner of Toronto's largest department retail chain.

Merinda sniffed. "That Tertius Montague could actually identify or name one of the many scullery maids in his employ is impressive. You're sure he's not the murderer?"

"It's too early to ascertain. He's at Station One for questioning."

Jem was still gaping at the woman in endless slumber splayed on the red carpet. She had an almost angelic stillness about her. "Surely it's time to move the body to the morgue."

"Oh, Jem, posh!" said Merinda. "If we removed the body to the morgue, we couldn't investigate the circumstances of the corpse in its surroundings. Search for clues!" Merinda dug into her vest pocket for a small magnifying glass and held it up against the hair of the deceased. It caught a prism of light from the theatre's modern fluorescent lighting scheme. Then she moved it slightly away to a small pile of ash.

---

* For *loitering*, read "waiting past dark at a streetcar stop."

"Morbid!" sighed Jem, following Merinda's gaze. "Someone smoking beside a dead body!"

"A left-handed person," added Merinda, stepping to the right and standing poised, mimicking lighting a cigar and holding it to her lips.

"The mortician will be here in a few minutes, Jem," Jasper said. "The police have finished their work here."

"Pish. The police miss everything obvious," Merinda said. "They probably even think this is the crime scene, when it must be clear to the greatest simpleton that she can't have been murdered here."

Jem and Jasper were silent.

"Oh, come," said Merinda. "What are the odds of her arms falling so neatly aligned with the line of her waist?"

Jasper looked at Merinda brightly. "Yes. Of course. Her arms are equally balanced on either side. No human could naturally fall into that position."

Merinda nodded. "So she was laid here. But why not hide the body? Conceal the murder? And there—feel her coat."

"It's damp," Jasper said. "I noticed when we were looking for identification."

"But it's not raining." Merinda crouched by the body and held up one of the girl's ivory hands.

"Maybe she was shoved in clothes just from the laundry," said Jem tentatively.

"Does she smell like she came from the laundry?" Merinda said. "Look here, Jasper!"

Jasper leaned in. The girl's fingernails had the slightest coating of dust. Merinda was about to expound on another theory when Jasper said, "Shhh!" and raised his hand.

They froze.

Jasper put a finger to his mouth and pushed them gently from the foyer, through the side of the auditorium, and to the backstage door at Victoria Street. He clicked it shut behind them as loud male voices broke the silence they'd left behind. It sounded like police talk.

"You two scurry," he said.

Merinda grabbed at Jasper's elbow and pulled tightly. "Please, Jasper, let me back in. I haven't finished investigating."

"No," Jasper said. "It'll be the end of my career if the sergeant finds out you were at the scene at all."

Merinda sighed. "Is Fiona…is the body going to the morgue now for an autopsy?"

"Yes, there will be an autopsy."

"And you'll keep us posted? You'll let us know what the autopsy shows?"

"Merinda, your excitement is indecent," Jem said. "A girl is dead."

"Shush, Jem! There's finally adventure at our fingertips, and I won't let it slip away." Merinda turned to the constable. "Jasper?" she entreated.

"Yes, yes. I'll loop you two in. Now, scurry!"

Ray DeLuca excelled at being at the right place at the wrong time. Today he was following Skip McCoy, the *Hogtown Herald's** sometimes photographer and all-around jack-of-all-trades, unaware the impromptu adventure would result in a corpse.

Skip had told him he knew a secret way up to the Winter Garden, the theatre atop the gilded Elgin Theatre, still several weeks away from its public opening. Later that night, the Elgin would be the scene of Montague's mayoral election rally. Everyone, including Montague's wealthy ally, Thaddeus Spenser, would be in attendance. Skip and Ray would kill a few hours, maybe find a diner nearby before staking out the crowd.

"Tertius Montague put some of his own money into the new theatre." Skip jumped up and wrestled with the ladder attached to the

---

* Canada's largest city acquired the moniker *Hogtown* in the previous century, borne of the sprawling stockyards of the Wm. Davies Company, one of the largest meatpackers in the country.

fire escape so it came clanking down with a thud. "Thaddeus Spenser contributed."

Ray looked left and right. Victoria Street was fairly empty for a sunny Saturday afternoon. He let ruddy-haired Skip get a head start and then pulled himself up after him, holding tightly to the handrails. A few flights and Skip opened the unlocked door.

Inside, Ray took off his bowler and muffed at his matted hair. Skip snaked a lit match along the brick wall until he found the lever and yanked so that the electric lights fizzled and spurted before they slowly lit. Their footsteps echoed in the cavernous backstage area, still in disarray. The workers must have had the morning off. Above, ropes and pulleys crisscrossed and drooped. In front, a black fire scrim barricaded them.

Ray maneuvered around piles of lumber and tarps to get nearer to Skip. "So you took me back here to see ropes and lanterns?" Ray replaced his hat, reached into his pocket, retrieved his father's pocket watch, and spun it around his finger.

"No, wait." Skip approached the fire scrim and Ray watched him peer around it. "All clear!" He motioned Ray over.

Ray followed and they stepped out onto the stage. Whatever lever Skip had pulled not only lit behind the curtain but the entirety of this garden-in-progress. Ray held his hand to his forehead.

It was a fairyland in the making. Even now, when it was just a phantom of soon-to-be-beauty, the leaves winding from the rafters and the painted vines and scalloped flora adorning the pillars and walls presaged its grandeur. Hundreds of painted twigs, birds, and fairy lanterns hung from real beech branches.

"How did you know this was up here?"

"I heard it around," Skip said vaguely.

"What are you doing here, Ray?" A man's voice came from the top of the grand staircase, the flights that wound down to the Elgin Theatre.

The voice was familiar to Ray. It was his brother-in-law. "Tony?"

"I asked what you're doing here."

"On a story." He threw a look at Skip.

"There's a corpse in the foyer," Tony said. "Pretty freckled girl with red hair almost as bright as the carpet."

Ray's eyes widened and Skip gasped.

"Did you put it there?" Ray asked lightly.

"Very funny."

"Then why are you here?"

Tony's face was in shadow. "Business for Montague."

"Let's go," said Skip. "If there's a girl dead downstairs we don't want to be found here."

Ray wanted to press further to determine what Tony's business was, but he heard footsteps—probably the police—ascending the staircase from below.

Ray and Skip exited the way they'd come in, agreeing on a time to meet later that evening.

Ray made his way to the streetcar stop and hopped on, tossing a coin at the driver, making his way to the back as the winking sunlight spread like an outsretched hand over the wide glass panes. His mind was full of a new story idea—one that McCormick, editor of the *Hogtown Herald*, hadn't even signed off on yet. St. Joseph's Home for Working Men: living conditions subsidized by Tertius Montague and Thaddeus Spenser.

The streetcar rambled on, a zigzag of telephone cables and wires overhead and a spark of wheels against the tracks underneath. To the sides the trenches were gutted, every street dug up, repaved, tracks hammered at a frantic pace, carriages squealing and almost colliding with automobiles.

Ray hopped off north of Elizabeth Street where St. Joseph's interrupted the sloping cottages and slanted houses of the Ward. Inside, light shone murkily through filmy windows and cracks snaked up the moldy wallpaper, exposing water-stained cement underneath.

He was greeted by a woman with strings of greasy gray hair falling over a pasty face. He flashed her a full-on smile and spoke in Italian, playing the part of the workingman. She handed him a ratty blanket and listed off the rules of the establishment, not seeming to care whether he understood English or not as she walked him to the common bunkroom. She didn't mention the fact that he had no belongings with him. He would learn later, watching men come in and out with nothing but the clothes on their backs, that this was customary.

"You're free to do as you like, but curfew is eleven and you must leave by eight the next morning. Eight, you understand?" She held up eight fingers. "Don't use the stove or the radiator or dry your socks there and never, ever entertain female company. Some of the men try to pass their *sisters* and *cousins* by me"—she turned to look at him pointedly—"but I know better."

He was left to settle in. As this required little more than flopping on his bed and removing his hat, he took the time to explore his surroundings. He peered through the window. The gated courtyard was more prison-like than Ray had anticipated. But prison or not, it was a place for men new to the country to spend a few nights, hoping there wasn't a long list for an empty bed and hoping they could secure a job the next morning to pay for bed and board.

Not long after, men shuffled in after their morning shift. It was a veritable Tower of Babel: All manner of languages sewed a tapestry of Yiddish, Italian, Chinese, and a few Nordic dialects. Ray creased open his journal, scribbling a few thoughts for his upcoming article. But despite all he saw around him, he had trouble focusing on anything other than the corpse at the theatre. Why would anyone murder someone there the same day as Montague's first campaign party—unless that was the reason for the murder in the first place?

Turning down his wrinkled blanket to mark his spot, he grabbed his coat and set out to meet Skip again.

❧

Jem wanted to take the streetcar from the theatre back to the residence she and Merinda shared at King Street, but Merinda was in no mood for the stifling crowds of the trolley. Assuring Jem that the fresh evening air would do their minds some good, Merinda set a frantic pace, straining ahead, her rapid stride made easier by the shortened length of her skirt.

Too short. The Morality Squad would write her a ticket if she wasn't careful.

For her part, Jem was dressed with decorum and decency and couldn't help but lag behind. In addition, Merinda's figure was far more lithe, with a boyish flatness of angles and lines, whereas Jem's soft, feminine curves filled out daysuits well but were not ideal for racing down to the West End at the speed of streetcars.

Autumn had rustled in with evenings as crisp as russet apples and skies a tangy cerulean blue. But the clear, bright days of September were all but behind them. Currently, showers threatened to burst from the low-hanging clouds, and the prospect of long, gloomy nights broken only by the flickering light of tallow candles stretched before them. The church bells of St. Andrews and St. James mixed with the whip of the wind in an eerie musical contest.

Finally, breathless and blistered, Merinda and Jem ascended the steps to their lodging. Merinda slid the key in the lock and opened the door while wriggling out of her coat. She tossed the coat on the floor, ignoring the glare it inspired from their landlady, Mrs. Malone, and stomped over the Persian rug in the front sitting room, bellowing for her Turkish coffee.

And thus they sat, causing Mrs. Malone to wonder loudly from the kitchen why two girls on the wrong side of twenty were oblivious to Toronto's numerous options for perfecting one's domestic skills and meeting appropriate young men. Especially when said girls were of such good breeding and high pedigree.

Mrs. Malone was not alone in her puzzlement. Jem wondered that too, constantly. Merinda was the most productively useless person she had ever met. Hardly ever gainfully employed, she spent hours in medical study at the university laboratory—despite the fact that she'd abandoned her plans to practice medicine. And she followed Jasper around like a dog promised a bone whenever there was a whiff of mystery in the air.

They kept their heads above the tide of impropriety—barely—thanks to Merinda's family's fortune and the watchful eye of Mrs. Malone. Jem felt the lack of romantic prospects more acutely. She had exchanged her parent's social circle for Merinda's odd moods, temper, and the air of constant excitement that followed them, especially when in the vicinity of a problem overseen by Jasper Forth. Merinda was so competitive in the company of the opposite sex that men had little choice but to cower. And she was oblivious to the way said police constable looked at her.

Back in university, the pair had been far more interested in the disappearance of a stolen watch or the conveniently circulating answers to a test than the realms of social and cordial respectability. Now they sat on either side of their hearth, another mystery buzzing at their fingertips, reliant on Jem's employment at Spenser's Department Store and Merinda's father's liberal allowance. Adrift on some urban island, marooned from respectable society.

Merinda couldn't have cared less. "Do you really think that Tertius Montague is the murderer? It seems too easy."

But Jem's mind was far away. "Do you ever wonder about security? About the future?" She thought about white picket fences and matching dishes from the Spenser's catalogue.

"Je-mi-ma!" Merinda said. "Do you think Montague is the murderer?"

"I wonder if we should go to one of those church socials," Jem said dreamily. "They have crokinole!"

"Cracker jacks, Jem! Sometimes I wonder if we are even having the same conversation. What about those hemp boys? The out-of-work sailors who work in the pullies? They could have used one of the ropes to strangle the girl."

"Silly sailors! Does it not bother you that my parents just dropped me like a hot poker?" She extracted the letter and pamphlet that had arrived in the morning's mail and waved them like a flag in front of her companion. "We have nothing to show for this mystery non-sense but a letter from the police congratulating you on a job well done...*for a woman!*"

"My dearest Jemima, do not be concerned about your future secu-rity. You know that I will always share whatever I have with you. Any-thing...from muffins to murder. Speaking of which...*Mrs. Malone! Where is my Turkish coffee?*" A tray and a pot and strainer materialized. "Thank you!" Her eyes lit. "Now, where were we?"

"You were going to find some form of useful employment," Jem said, reaching for a cup, "and we were both going to pursue appro-priate feminine activity."

"Oh, absolutely not! We're going to Tertius Montague's elec-tion rally, of course. It's been in the papers for weeks—he's giving a speech, and everyone who matters in Toronto is invited, including your esteemed employer, Mr. Thaddeus Spenser. I suppose the police will let poor Montague out of questioning long enough to attend his own fund-raiser. He'll want to use it to clear his name." She jumped up, pacing on the Persian rug. "I'm going to need you to be my out-side ears and eyes. I'll go inside, of course. I am much better prepared to mingle with the higher echelons of society."

"You have the worst manners of anyone I have ever met!"

Merinda bounded from the room. "Trousers, vests, and bowl-ers, Jemima!"

CHAPTER TWO

*There is no dignity in solving mysteries. You
will, eventually, in the pursuit of solution,
learn that efficiency is more important
than pride in appearance or form.*

Guide to the Criminal and Commonplace, M.C. Wheaton

Jem realized early in her acquaintance with Merinda Herringford
that attempting to solve a crime as an amateur and a woman
meant leaving any semblance of pride or dignity behind. She
became all too familiar with hiding her attractive feminine traits—
her soft curves and curls—under the dirty, mangy tweed folds of her
flatmate's nifty disguises.

They kept those disguises in a trunk in Merinda's bedroom. It
contained castoffs from Merinda's uncle—a former actor whom Jem
liked to picture rambling about the countryside in a traveling troupe
performing second-rate Shakespeare. The most-used garments were
trousers, bowlers, and vests, all of which would have caused Jem's parents to pale to the color of death. But they were necessary to avoid
the unwanted attention of the Morality Squad. Two strolling females
would call too much attention to themselves, and would even face
the prospect of jail.

Having lost her best pair of trousers to one of Merinda's recent
chemical experiments, Jem was worried as she held up the alternative
in front of her: a pair of never-before-worn monstrous pinstripes that
threatened to fall down the moment she took a single step.

"Women walk with their hips," Merinda said, the false moustaches on her upper lip giving a deft twirl to her mouth. "But men walk with their legs." She demonstrated, her boots and long pants stretching out in a display of exaggerated masculinity.*

Jem tried to emulate her stance and stride, feeling generally lucky to escape the eyebrow makeup and moustaches. Instead, her fair features were blemished with grease and grime while Merinda adorned her with a wig, unkempt strands sprouting in all directions. Jem was close to letting Merinda strap a pillow to her stomach to round out the oversized clothes, but Merinda settled on having her look lanky, as if she was unable to keep enough food in her belly to hold her belt buckle straight.

"These pants will not stay up, Merinda," Jem said at the doorway.

"Perfect!" Merinda clapped.

"I am warning you, they will fall down to my knees."

"Then you'll look destitute. Poor waif! Can't even afford pants that fit."

Merinda's garb was distinctly upper crust. She practiced the smirk of the rich: smugly self-satisfied, with a chin tilted at the rest of the world.

Jem thought of a dozen ways this scheme would fail, but she didn't relay them to Merinda. Instead, she resigned herself to wait outside the event, hovering by a lamppost with her knees pulled to her chin, cursing her fate, while Merinda was inside, silver clattering and champagne glasses tinkling.

She breathed a prayer for the rain to hold off and to avoid detection, at which Merinda smirked, scolding her friend for conversing with an invisible God. But He wasn't invisible to Jem, and there were some things that even the great Merinda Herringford didn't control.

Ten minutes later, Jem waddled down the street, wondering how to keep her pants from falling down. Merinda turned every few paces

---

* If female readers are under the impression that walking without moving one's hips is easy, they are encouraged to try it sometime.

to remind Jem to emulate her masculine stance and stride. She was answered with a dozen angry looks shot from under the flickering streetlights.

Easy for her, Jem thought. Merinda's pants fit her perfectly. The curve of Jem's hips and the incline of her waist did not suit the trousers. She hiked them up as best she could and, upon reaching the threshold of bustling Yonge Street, hoped she just looked like some intoxicated old fool.

Merinda marched forward in the direction of the Elgin Theatre, rapping her walking stick, which if necessary could double as a crowbar, in punctuated rhythm with her quick pace. As they reached the intersection, she shoved Jem back. "We cannot be seen together anymore." Her overdrawn eyebrows settled into an exaggerated furrow.

Jem's whisper back was exasperated: "So what do you want me to do?"

"Use your powers of memory. I want you to be able to recall details of everyone who enters. Note who bends down to throw pennies at you in your pathetic state. Note—"

"My pathetic state! I'm only pathetic because—"

"Quiet! And if you see anyone who doesn't look like they belong here—besides yourself, of course—let me know about it."

Merinda began to turn away but Jem clutched at her coat sleeve. "How am I supposed to know who belongs and who doesn't?"

"Use your intuition. I need to be inside, so you're my eyes and ears out here. We need to find something on Tertius Montague so Jasper will let us be part of it. Part of it all."

"What do you think you can possibly find at an event meant to celebrate the mayor?"

"Anything suspicious. The man was just held for questioning for the murder of a girl in his beautiful theatre. Even though I stand by my belief that the murder took place somewhere else entirely. If he's guilty, something will show. And if he's in league with someone else, who knows who will filter in and out of the crowd? Now go." She shoved Jem. "Go beg for alms like a good girl."

Jem watched Merinda disappear, and she shuffled over the pavement, finally settling by a lamppost near the entrance to the theatre. Merinda was soon lost in a sea of other black coattails. Ladies flitted by Jem, their skirts brushing her with swooshes of satin and lace. Gentlemen looked down with sneers and snarls. A few tried to shoo her away—a rapscallion who would somehow tarnish their evening.

A few men dipped into their pockets and the ladies their handbags, fishing out coins that Jem acknowledged in a deep voice. Her hat started looking rather full, inspiring her to wonder if she had chosen the wrong career as a Spenser's department store mailroom girl.

Certainly the upper echelons of society in front of her, glistening and ornamented, could spare the change they tossed into her overturned hat. Nonetheless, Jem's conscience pricked her, and she decided she would put the spoils in the St. James poor box at the end of the evening.

Finally, most of the crowd was inside, and golden-hued beams of warmth spilled through the ornate doorframes. Jem had little to do then but watch the clouds—which were looking more ominous every minute—and hope to be spared a downpour. She sat clinking the change in her cap and wondering what Sherlock Holmes would do.

Observation: The polished handle of a walking stick. The scuff on a shoe. A woman wringing her hands as she looks up, besotted, at the man beside her. A man casting a longing glance at his friend's companion while another woman, dour and severe, settles her gloved hand into the crook of his arm.

The muffled cello section of a Bach piece slipped through the broad doors, and Jem thought of Merinda inside. Thus a half hour elapsed with Jem sitting and shivering, jangling her coins and watching for anything suspicious or interesting. Couples began meandering outside to take in the night air, dresses and coattails brushing side by side. Snatches of music followed them.

Jem was in the process of moving the most recent collection of change from her hat to her breast pocket when she noticed someone crouched at her level. His black hair was just barely contained by the circumference of a ratty old bowler, and decidedly charcoal eyes were piercing her straight on.

"Excuse me."

Was he addressing her? She growled something inaudible in a lower octave of voice and then added a quick *yes*, hoping it sounded masculine. Unfortunately, it came out squeaking and high, and she slapped her palm over her mouth.

"Have you been sitting here long?"

Jem nodded. Shook her head. And fairly gaped as he sat down beside her.

"Isn't this the way? The rich inside at a charity ball, dolling out twenty-five dollars a ticket to aid the illustrious Tertius Montague, while mostly tripping over you, poor fellow, right in front of their noses."

Jem wanted to protest but was afraid her voice would betray her even further. Instead she glared at the man, hoping her disguise would stand the test of such close proximity. His black eyes looked everywhere, as if drinking in the whole scene at once.

"I want you to know," he was saying, "that I advocate for charity, yes, but I also want to give a voice to people like you! People who are just ordinary, under the noses of the upper crust who pass callously by. People who"—he examined her thoroughly, closely—"people who..." The man clapped his hands on his knees. "*Santo cielo!*"

"Shhh!"

He laughed. "You're a woman!"

"I'm not a woman!" Jem sounded very, very much like a woman.

"There are places for people like you. Safe places. Get you off the street. Do you want to get arrested?" He clapped his hands on his knees again and fidgeted in his coat pocket to retrieve a notebook and pencil stub. "Ray DeLuca of the *Hogtown Herald*." He extended his free hand.

The *Hogtown Herald*. Jem recognized the name of the biweekly rag, commonly called the *Hog*, which was filled with this fellow's muckraking exposés on the city's lack of social justice and reform. When she didn't take his hand, he grabbed hers anyway and shook it hard. She noticed his nails: They were coal black, as black as his eyes and hair. "I'm trying to get the perspective of the street people. Especially in contrast to big parties like this."

"Oh, rats!"

"Do you find that you make more money with that disguise?"

"I am not a woman!"

"I don't believe you!" He reached up and yanked off her hat, and a pile of brown hair fell around her shoulders. "You're the oddest hobo I've ever met. If we could just get that grime off your face. Now, Miss...Miss..."

Jem buried her face in her hands. This was awful. "Watts."

"Excuse me? You're muttering."

"Miss Jemima Watts."

"Ready for your interview, Miss Watts?"

"No!" Jem leapt to her feet, almost leaving her pants behind. She hitched her fingers into the belt loops, pulled them high over her bloomers, and strode away.

Ray jumped up and followed. "Oh, come now, Miss Watts. I need a story, and you need something to distract you from the fact that it is going to pour down rain any second."

A heavy raindrop pierced her eyelash. "Rats!"

"You said that already." There was a smile in his heavily accented voice.

"I'm going home!"

"Home? Then you're a fraud. You're not a street person at all! Why is a young woman dressed like a hobo mounting the steps of the city's most highbrow event? Are you a spy?" His black eyes twinkled.

"Let me go."

She elbowed past him just as thunder crashed and the sky broke. Water came down in heavy sheets, and her pants finally gave way, leaving her in nothing but lace bloomers and heavy stockings. Mortified, she watched as the pants puddled around her ankles.

Ray watched with interest before remembering his gentlemanly manners and turning away. She asked him for a handkerchief, demurely accepting the one he held out and wiping the makeup off her face. The girl was trembling like an agitated bunny and so very wet. He wriggled out of his overcoat and offered it. "Here."

She wrapped it around herself and muffled something that sounded a bit like a thank-you. Then she fell on the side of the pillar and laughed.

Merinda was bored out of her socks. Sure, the broad imitation marble columns and platinum leaves, damask wall fabric, high mirrors, and polished banister of the grand staircase were a sight to behold. Especially as Tertius Montague's prepossessing and surprisingly calm figure appeared at the top. He made his way down while his men kept the reporters at bay. Camera bulbs flashed and sparked.

Montague raised a hand and began, slowly, to speak. "This is Toronto's century," he said, "and it will be a city constantly in motion." He proceeded to speak about his plans for the theatre in which they stood. Vaudeville acts and even moving pictures. Soon, very soon, the grand opening of the Winter Garden Theatre atop the elegant Elgin would come, and he promised that it would take everyone's breath away.

Merinda leaned against her walking stick and yawned as Montague filled the air with his boasts. Indeed, it got interesting only when a flame-haired and red-faced young man burst from behind a waiter and pushed his way through the crowd, tears in his eyes and vengeance in his voice.

"How dare you!" he screamed, persistent even as men grabbed his arms and restrained him. "Here, in the very place Fiona died! Probably by your hand."

"Look here, you ruffian," Montague began.

"Ruffian! Name's Fred O'Hare. Fiona was to be my wife."

Merinda's eyes followed the dignitaries and officials to watch their reaction. In the corner, she noticed a man leaning lackadaisically against one of the marble columns. She recognized Gavin Crawley, reporter for the *Globe and Mail.* He had, she remembered, a bit of a reputation as a ladies' man.

"You're a murderer!" the young man was shouting. He pulled a gun from his coat pocket.

Chief of Police Henry Tipton's voice filled the foyer. "Apprehend him, men!"

Officers surged forward and restrained the young man. He was subdued and carted off the premises. The gun was left behind.

Chief Tipton turned to look at the crowd and shook his head. "I'm sure you've all heard about the unfortunate young woman whose body was discovered here earlier. But there is no evidence to suggest that anyone here murdered that poor girl. Pray, let's continue with the purpose of the evening and our support of Montague's campaign."

Convenient, Merinda thought while staring at Montague's smug smile, to have the Chief of Police on your side.

But before Montague could continue with his practiced speech, a loud commotion erupted from the direction of the powder room. Merinda quickly moved in the direction of the crowd and was there when the first panicked announcement of a corpse in the ladies' room made its way over in terrified succession.

Merinda meandered through the milling throng out the doors, shoving past women pressing smelling salts to their noses and weeping into the coat sleeves of their gentleman companions.

She found Jem breathless, stocking-clad legs sticking out from the ends of a man's overcoat, makeup wiped away, and hair down around her face.

"Jem! Jem! It's a good thing we're here! There's another body."

❧

Merinda had read too many penny dreadfuls and had spent too much time with Mr. Doyle's stories not to dash back to the scene of the crime.

To her chagrin, Merinda found it difficult to get close enough to inspect the dead girl. But the whispers erupting around her confirmed that it was, again, strangulation.

Jem, still folded in the *Hog* reporter's overcoat, searched the room and saw Ray DeLuca, just briefly, in much clearer light. Since he was now coatless and under the lamplight, it was easier to note how his hair shone under the decorative gas lanterns.

She wondered if he was looking for her to reclaim his coat, but he seemed preoccupied and agitated. Fortunately, the commotion over the body's discovery meant she could slide around unnoticed despite her horrid appearance.

"They're connected." Merinda elbowed closer to the corpse, tugging Jem with her. "These murders. They're connected."

"I have to return that reporter's coat," said Jem. "Though I suppose if I take it off, half of Toronto will notice I have no pants on."

Merinda gave her an inscrutable look before returning to her inspection of the hall.

Several bluecoats from the Toronto Metropolitan Police entered, parting the crowd to circle the victim. Jem and Merinda were thus left on the sidelines without the privilege Jasper had afforded them earlier that day.

Defeated, Merinda pointed toward the door and they stepped into the chill of the autumn air. Rain spattered the pavement. Merinda found what was probably the only vacant cab in a mile's radius and whistled for it.

The wheels hissed over the damp pavement. Jem slid into the back of the automobile first, not wanting to spend one more moment with only the reporter's coat keeping her from the wind. She would have to get it back to him somehow. Jem suspected Merinda would have a dozen or so questions about her state of undress and the events of the evening. Happy that the darkness shaded the blush that had yet to leave her face, Jem rode in silence. But Merinda's brain was turning so quickly Jem could almost hear it.

Chapter Three

Never be too eager to leave the scene of a crime. It might be tempting when other parties, such as the police, arrive to pursue their own investigation, but the astute detective will stalwartly search out every last inch of the perimeter in question and not be deterred by other human activity around them.

Guide to the Criminal and Commonplace, M.C. Wheaton

COATLESS, SOAKED REPORTER PURSUES DEADBEAT, DRUNKEN BROTHER-IN-LAW HALFWAY AROUND TORONTO.

It wasn't nearly as compelling as GIRLS DRESSED AS MEN HOVER IN DISGUISE AT CRIME SCENE, but it would have to do for now.

Back inside, Ray DeLuca hooked his thumbs in his suspenders and hoped his mind was playing tricks on him. He would swear he had seen someone he shouldn't have.

Skip McCoy, red hair tumbling over his forehead, asked him what photographs he should attempt to take first.

"Snap it all, Skip," Ray said absently, his eyes roaming the foyer of the theatre. Skip began to carry out his assignment, but Ray sprang down the steps and into the downpour again, giving up what might have been an interesting piece on a girl in disguise and her corpse-discovering friend—also female, he suspected, on account of the voice contradicting her dark moustaches—in exchange for the pursuit of his drunk and deadbeat brother-in-law.

MAYOR MONTAGUE AND THE CASE OF THE SECOND CORPSE, he mused as he followed Tony through the rain.

Ray stopped at a corner and blinked away the raindrops. Tony was gone. Ray crossed back to College Street, swerving between a few horse-drawn carriages and a honking automobile before he stopped for breath. He swished his bowler off his head, punched it in its oft-punched center, and ran his fingers through his black hair.

Ray desperately wanted to hop in the next cab, forget about the bed he had claimed at St. Joseph's, and retreat to his room on Trinity Street, where he would sink into dry clothes and recount the day in his journal. But he couldn't, not with Tony's sudden appearance at the scene of the crime. Or so his eyes had told him.

He loped along in a slow jog, heading to the entrance to St. John's Ward, a central neighborhood spilling over with immigrants, vagrants, run-down housing, and ill-swept streets. At the very mouth of Elizabeth Street sat the tiny ramshackle cottage his sister, Viola, and her oft-drunk husband shared.

Ray had to rap on the doorframe twice before Viola appeared in the soft lantern light of her front sitting room.

"You're sure it was Tony?" she asked as she listened to her brother's story, punctuated with a few colorful words in their native language.

"Can you at least let me in?" Ray shook the water out of his hair. Viola stood to one side of the cottage door. "I'm going to stay the night," he said.

"That's not necessary."

"I am staying until Tony arrives. When do you expect him home? Why was he at the Elgin, Vi? What work is he doing?"

"He works odd jobs for Mayor Montague. You know that."

Ray stepped out of his shoes and plopped onto the mismatched cushions of the sagging sofa. Viola's home was threadbare. The wind whistled too liberally through the cracks of the roof and the rain spattered into a bucket in the middle of the sitting room, but the cottage succumbed the best it could to her domestic pride.

"Where is your coat?" Viola took her brother's bowler hat and dabbed at it with a towel.

"I did something chivalrous and loaned it to a girl. And then I saw Tony. Somewhere I shouldn't have seen him. This is becoming a habit."

Viola tugged her shawl more tightly around her nightgown. "Must you stay the night, Ray? I hate it when the two of you get in a row."

"We get in a row because I can't stand to see him treat you the way he does." Ray inclined his head in the direction of the cottage's single bedroom, if one could call it that. It was a corner of the home partitioned off by a ratty blanket that offered minimal privacy from the living area and the kitchen's sputtering stove. There, he knew, slept his nephew, Luca, a little boy who would be half-starved alongside his mother if Ray didn't subsidize Tony's sporadic income with some of his own.

"He's trying."

Ray stifled his first response. "Vi, I want to know why he is working for Mayor Montague. He certainly doesn't work on the books. It's common knowledge that Montague pays men under the table for performing…less than legal jobs. How else could he run half the city? One of the men at the Don Jail* told me all about it. He said…"

"Not the Don Jail again, Ray."

"And who knows what Tony does to scrape up his liquor money?"

"You hurt my feelings." Viola's long, purple-black curls fell haphazardly around her face, much as they had done when she'd been a little girl.

She looked more and more like a little girl each day, Ray thought—cornered, cajoled, and beaten down by her husband. Ray intervened as much as he could, but Viola loved Tony, so coming to fisticuffs with him resulted in little more than black eyes and more tears for his sister.

---

* A year earlier, Ray DeLuca had feigned arrest to be tossed in a cell at the Don Jail with a poor excuse for a trial. From its depths, he investigated the unfair treatment of the prisoners there. Along the way, he learned how easy it was to bribe guards—and to get a sentence cut short by being affiliated with Mayor Tertius Montague.

Viola's English was far poorer than Ray's, and she lapsed into Italian now. She defended Tony as she always did, explaining how hard it had been for him to adjust to their new life in Canada. He hadn't always been this way. He would be himself again someday. But even after five years in the country, these Canadian men didn't give him a chance.

"You make your own chance here, Vi. You have to make your own chance."

"I'm tired. You woke me up." She clicked her tongue. "Look at you. You're soaked to the bone. I will make you some tea."

She moved toward the stove and put a kettle on to boil. "Here. Put this on." She took one of Tony's cable-knit sweaters from the clothes-line strung across the ceiling over the dinner table. Ray turned his back to her, wrestled out of his soaked shirt, and settled into the warm woolen folds of Tony's sweater.

He was much more comfortable now, especially with a cup of hot tea. He told Vi about the funny girl who had his coat. "The worst part is, I left my notebook in the pocket. It just dawned on me that I don't have it."

"What a strange girl." Viola wrinkled her nose. "Going about begging."

He didn't want to come back around to Tony, but it was inevitable. "Then I saw Tony and I had to leave her there without explanation."

"Did Tony see you?"

"Not that I know of."

"Good." Viola grabbed the fabric of Ray's sweater and tugged him closer. "I want you two to get along. Like in the old days."

Ray tried to smile. "I worry about you."

"I worry about you too." She sipped tea from a cracked china cup. "When was the last time you went to confession? Father Byrne said you haven't been 'round in weeks."

Ray looked for something to settle his eyes on. There was a week-old copy of the *Globe and Mail* on the side table. The headline written by golden-boy Gavin Crawley. What with his all-Canadian pedigree and looks, British family, and inherited money, Crawley didn't have to scrape by at a third-rate paper like Ray did. "I haven't been to confession, no."

"Or mass?"

"I go to a different mass."

"You don't go to St. Paul's at all anymore, do you?" Viola's brow furrowed and she crossed herself. Their deceased mother would turn over in her grave.

Ray started at the thought of the gorgeous cathedral in the heart of Corktown. "I haven't been going to mass for a long time."

The door creaked open on its rusty hinges, and they both turned at the sound. Tony appeared, drenched and stumbling. Viola ran to get a towel while Ray concentrated on swallowing his temper. His fists were so tightly pressed that he felt the crescents of his fingernails digging into his palms.

Tony's eyes widened at Ray. "What are you doing here?"

Ray narrowed his eyes. "What were you doing at the Elgin Theatre today where that girl was murdered?"

Viola gasped loudly. "Stop!"

"Shhh!" Tony hissed. "You'll wake the boy and I'll get no sleep! And take off my sweater."

"You're drunk, Tony." Viola's voice was soft.

Ray clenched his teeth. "You're surprised?"

"Get your useless brother out of my house." Tony edged by Viola and crashed around in the kitchen until he found a half-full bottle of whiskey. He popped the cap and took a swig.

"Stop!" Viola pleaded. "Stop. This drinking is why Ray is here. This is why you go off and end up where a girl has been killed. Stop." She reached out, tugging at the bottle. Tony held fast to it while shoving her back with his free hand. Viola toppled against the counter.

Ray looked up at Tony. His jaw hurt from clenching, and every sinew in his body ached from being suppressed. He looped back his arm and let loose a swing.

Merinda and Jem thawed themselves in front of the fire. Jem could tell that Merinda was puzzling out the connection between the two murdered women. But Jem's mind was on herself and her embarrassing performance, which had culminated in losing her trousers in front of that DeLuca fellow. Who, most likely, would skewer it across the morning headlines. She played the scene over and over again, and each time it was more humiliating. This was the first man who had ever seen her without layers of a carefully constructed feminine cage, and she flushed and sank lower into her chair at the thought. How had she looked? Were her thighs too thick? Her waist too thin?

She still had the reporter's coat folded over her arm. She lifted it to her nose and inhaled. It was a piney hybrid of outdoors, sweat, and rain. She allowed her truant fingers to find their way into the pockets.

A notebook. She impulsively removed it.

"You've got the right idea, Jem!" Merinda snatched one end of the coat. "Let's go exploring." Merinda found a pocket watch in the tawny folds of the other pocket.

"Clues?" Jem said. "But the reporter was just there for the speech. He can't have been involved in the murders." She sniffed again, deeply. "It smells like the city. The lapping harbor, the steam and grime of the wharfs, the overcrowded stench of the Ward. A soft fall breeze."

"You can smell all that? Oh, look!" Merinda excavated a pencil nub and snatched the coat to her side of the hearth. "I wonder what he was doing there. Did your trousers fall off in front of a murderer?"

Jem was absently inspecting her fingers. "Mmm?"

"What's that black stuff on your hand?"

"It's ink. His fingernails were black with it. He shook my hand and left some on me. I told you, he's not the murderer. He's a reporter."

"The coat is very old. Threadbare, almost. And I don't think he was the original owner. I only saw him for a moment, but he's a medium-sized man, and this coat is barely large enough for you. I don't think it's his."

"Does it matter?"

"Well, if he killed someone, maybe he left his coat and took this one instead."

"Poor Ray DeLuca," Jem said with a laugh, "unaware he is the subject of your irrational presumptions."

"Ray DeLuca? That was Ray DeLuca?"

Jem's eyes widened. "You know him?"

"He's that fellow from the *Hog*."

"You read the *Hog*?"

"Yes, I read the *Hog*," said Merinda. "He wrote a long muckraking piece on the Don Jail. I like him. He hates the Morality Squad. Too bad he might be a murderer."

"I told you, he's not."

But Merinda was no longer listening. Turning the pocket watch over in her hands, she brought the coat out to the kitchen. "Something for the laundry, Mrs. Malone," Jem heard her say.

"Sherlock Holmes discovers a lot from a pocket watch in *The Sign of the Four*," Merinda said as she returned to the sitting room. "Silver. A bit tarnished. And look—something written on the back. Can't read it." She tossed the watch to Jem, who caught it handily.

"Italian," said Jem, looking at the inscription. She flipped the watch open and heard its beguiling tick. A picture of a pretty woman and a little boy was pasted just inside.

Jem looked at it and blinked a few times. "His wi—Well, his family."

"You're acting very strange this evening, Jemima." Merinda took the watch back and closed it. "The journal seems more interesting than this old thing." She motioned for Jem to pass it over. Pasted on the front flap was another sentimental memento, a grainy picture of two children, the sun stretched behind them. Merinda didn't give it more than a moment's thought before turning the first pages.

Jem felt more than a little guilty as Merinda began reading Ray DeLuca's thoughts aloud.

Merinda opened to a page full of flowery thoughts about a girl named Angelica. Half in Italian. She snorted and moved on. There was nothing in the book about Ray's wife and child, but there were pages and pages about a sister and nephew—most likely, Merinda decided, the people in the watch photograph.

Finally, there was the material about the Don Jail. He had detailed events and descriptions that Merinda remembered reading about in Ray's *Hogtown Herald* pieces. Other aspects he'd recorded about the jail were even more disturbing, and Jem felt as if she were exhuming a sordid new underworld she had never imagined.

> **DAY ONE.** Incarcerated. McCormick wants me to go muckraking on account of there being little news other than the rumored and abhorrent conditions here. Blasted newspaper editors! I offered to help. But carrying through with that offer means mold, lice, dirt and a horrible mixture of watery oats that constitutes dinner.

> **DAY THREE.** Hungry as I was on the passage, and I remember that gnawing ghost pain.

Merinda stopped and moved to the chalkboard beside their hearth. It was used for everything from grocery lists to Jemima's work schedule and a few chemistry problems she and Jasper were trying to crack on weekends. She wiped it clean with her sleeve and began a list of suspects:

Ray DeLuca
Tertius Montague
Fred O'Hare

"Fred O'Hare?" Jem asked, reading the unfamiliar name.

"Fiona's fiancé. He was at the rally tonight."

Jem took up the journal and continued reading aloud:

> My bunkmate is a fellow named Forbes. He is known to me through my brother-in-law, Tony. The flat tick we sleep on is little more than a hard slat. And his bulk spills over the sides.

DAY SEVEN. I want to hear the St. James church bells.

DAY EIGHT. My first visitor arrived today. Constable Forth.

Jem and Merinda locked eyes. Merinda took the journal and read it aloud.

He pulled a favor so he could come and sit on the opposite side of the bars. I have met him a few times. That amiable face of his was the brightest thing I've seen in the Don since I arrived.

He could give me only crumbs of news. He checked on Viola and Luca for me, like the solid man he is. His mother offered to watch Luca while Viola looked for work. He brought them cookies and bread. This man—a stranger—takes better care of them than Tony does.

DAY NINE. Viola sent a tear-spattered note. She's sure I'm on the peg for something I was driven to do out of poverty from supporting her. I wonder if Tony receives the same heartbreak every time he's tossed in jail after a drunken rage somewhere.

DAY TEN. The fellow on the other side of the cell is rambling. I can make out his face just barely in the slight shaft of sunlight. He might be drunk. He lights up a cigar. He's talking about flowers from his garden. Flowers he cut for a girl. She's not good for him, he tells me. He's stuttering a little. Probably a nervous habit. He asks me, half-mad, if I knew of a path under Yonge that connects the old bank to the Massey Hall. I thought that tunnel was a legend. He's rambling about the Count of Monte Cristo and how he could escape. He knows about tunnels. They were built in the 1812 war in case of a siege.

He doesn't sound like the others here. He's a bit of a dandy. Muttering something about the Ward. Got a girl in trouble. It's a story I've heard countless times before. Then he starts on again about his knowledge of the Dominion Bank. There's a tunnel there that stretches from under it to the Massey Hall on Shuter Street. I've sketched it in my mind. It was the most amusing thing I've heard in days…

Day Twenty-one. It's fortunate Constable Forth's mother has been kind to Viola. For, currently, Tony is in the Don as well. Seems to know my bunkmate, Forbes, quite well. He broke into Spenser's. Heaven knows what he wanted from a department store. Well, I know that whatever the reason for his crime, it was farmed for a pretty penny. Sad how the same story plays over and over. It seems those of darkest hearts and cleanest hands know exactly who to prey upon for a fast dollar.

I watch Tony and think of the little boy who once played jacks with me by the river. He's still pleasant enough when he laughs. But he rarely laughs. Life in America was supposed to be better for us, but it has taken all the lightness from him.

Merinda closed the journal. "This gives a little more depth to those Don Jail articles, eh?"

They said good night, and Jem ascended the steps, performed her evening toilette, and went to bed. And there, tucked beneath her floral eiderdown, she explored Ray DeLuca's journal more carefully.

From her brief encounter with him, she had not imagined he would have such delicate handwriting. She brightened the lamp on her side table and flipped through the thin pages. She read his notes, dated and detailing the scenarios of the day as well as appointments and ideas for articles. Some entries were difficult to understand, and some involved a shorthand code of names and places.

This Ray DeLuca was a reformer, as was evident through his observations on the horrid conditions of St. John's Ward. Some pages bore nothing but quotations and overheard statements of a judicial, legal, or municipal tone. And there were even a few poems—terrible ones, she was forced to admit—in the style of Wordsworth. They were ill-fitting, like his coat, Jem observed.

Reading his notebook was like reading a cadence of the city. It was a strange little book, this collection of thoughts and poems and scribblings. Jem's favorite aspect of it was the running lexicon he kept in the back pages, proof that English still presented a challenge: *Beguiled. Ornery. Significant. Precipice. Cumulonimbus.*

She bit back her smile, and with a jumble of vocabulary words lolling around in her head, she fell fast asleep.

CHAPTER FOUR

Who is the Corktown Murderer?" Jem read Gavin Crawley's byline from the breakfast table.

Merinda swallowed a large bite of toast and marmalade. "The Corktown Murderer?"

"Both the murdered girls were from Corktown—most of the Irish immigrants live there," said Jem. "Fiona Byrne and Grace Kennedy. Sound decidedly Irish to me."

"And you look decidedly dreadful. Did you sleep at all last night?"

Jem's mouth dropped open, but she was spared from having to form a reply by Mrs. Malone's voice coming from the doorway. "Constable Forth is here."

Jasper stepped into the kitchen wearing civilian clothes. His blue eyes were highlighted by purple rings of fatigue.

"Speaking of decidedly dreadful," Merinda mumbled from the side of her mouth. "Coffee, Jasper?"

Jasper smiled weakly and took the chair she offered him. She poured and plopped in two lumps of sugar and a dribble of cream. Just the way she liked it.

"Now, Jasper," Merinda said, "we are going to need you to arrest Ray DeLuca."

Jem suppressed surprise.

Jasper tested the coffee. "That muckraker from the *Hog*?"

"Yes."

"Why?"

"He saw Jem *en déshabille* and she has been up half the night worrying that she will be his next headline in that silly *Hog* newspaper." Merinda didn't mention they had been rifling through his journal.

"Merinda," cried Jem, "that is not true."

"Nonsense. I deduced. Look at you."

Jem slumped a little lower in her chair.

"I can't arrest anyone right now, unfortunately," said Jasper, patting his street clothes. "We were found out, girls. Someone reported my letting you near the first body. And I am off the case. The Corktown case. Any case. Temporary demotion. I'm back on the traffic squad."

Merinda moaned. "That's no use to me!"

"And you both need to stop bounding about in pants. That band of moralizers is cracking the whip hard. I never should've taken you to the Elgin. Now look where it's got me." Jasper ruefully inspected his coffee cup.

"What's your new beat?" Jem asked gently.

"King and Yonge. Worst intersection in the city. And there's threat of a trolley strike."

Jem and Merinda exchanged an empathetic glance.

"I am terribly sorry, Jasper." Jem placed her hand over his. "It's a rotten business, and we never should have been there in the first place."

"Thank you, Jemima." He seemed to be waiting for Merinda to extend the same sympathies, but judging from her expression, she was miles away.

They lingered a few moments longer, Jasper in no great hurry to return to the King and Yonge beat, until Jemima had to begin preparing for work. She tucked a pressed shirtwaist into her best black skirt and headed out for Spenser's Department Store.

Settled on the streetcar, Jem spent her short commute peeking into Ray's journal again, looking up sheepishly now and then on the off-chance that its owner was nearby.

> DAY TWENTY-TWO. Tony won't quit talking about Spenser. They tell me he deserved to be robbed. They have heard no end from their friends in the warehouse of how he mistreats his employees and will do anything to dock pay or keep from having to dole out the money his workers are owed. I tell them there are better ways to get something done, but they wonder how you can get the attention of someone who won't hear you other than to take back what is rightfully yours.

Jem snapped the book shut as the driver called her stop. She alighted and crossed Yonge to the stories-high red brick of Spenser's, admiring the opulent window displays as she walked down Queen Street to the employee entrance.

Her initial employment at Spenser's Department Store had been as a mailroom girl. She'd spent eight hours a day opening letters from catalogue subscribers and sending them to the order room to be processed and filled. Then there came a promotion, of sorts, to the packaging room, which was overseen by a surly foreman with a slick handlebar moustache. There with Tippy Carr, a slight blonde girl with doe eyes and a button nose, Jem giftwrapped packages and tied them with sateen ribbon. Jem was dedicated to her job—she needed the money, after all—but Tippy bordered on obsession.

As the day progressed, Jem watched the clock. She watched it even more intently after three, aching to shrug into her coat and leave.

Finally, five o'clock came and their shift ended. Jem sprang away from their table, but Tippy lingered.

"You go on without me."

Jem knew that Tippy lived near Corktown and had little family to go home to. But she also knew that Tippy, more in need of the pay than Jem was, didn't receive any overtime checks or goodwill from her long shifts. So why stay?

Jem turned toward home, a little apprehensive as she saw newsies hawking the evening edition of the *Hog*. Would Ray DeLuca have found a way to work their humiliating meeting into a headline?

She bought a copy of the *Hog* from a newsboy and flipped through it. Unless she missed it, there was nothing at all about a strange trouser-less girl.

Jem breathed relief as she trudged up the stairs to their flat. She passed the paper to Merinda, who demanded it as soon as she spotted it tucked under her friend's arm.

"Well." Merinda stretched her legs out on the Persian carpet as she read. "He didn't get much more last night than any of the other reporters." She waved a hand over several other newspapers strewn around the floor. Merinda had been examining them—quite closely, it would appear—since Jem had left for her shift that morning.

"Is there anything of interest?"

Merinda stretched. "I think the only thing of interest is the fact that Jasper is back on street patrol."

"Poor Jasper. That *is* awful. We ought to do something."

"Send a fruit basket?" Merinda huffed. "It's rotten luck for us. With Jasper gone, they won't throw us any good mysteries, and *then* what will we do with our time?" She flicked a fanned-out paper with the tip of her shoe.

"You could find a job."

"Serious suggestions only, please." She tilted her head. "Besides, I have a job. I am an investigator."

Jem studied the paper and bit her tongue. Nothing could come from pointing out that it didn't count as a job unless one was paid.

Instead, she commented about her coworker. "Tippy was in a strange mood today."

Sometimes Tippy came over for dinner or tea after a long day. Occasionally, the three went to see a Nickelodeon.

But Merinda wasn't paying attention. Something about the pictures of the young man holding a gun at the election party had caught her eye. "Fred O'Hare."

"Who?"

"I told you last night. Fiona Byrne's fiancé." She pointed, and Jem looked at the caption identifying him.

"What about him?"

Merinda skimmed the article and then looked up. "Get your things. We're going."

Fred O'Hare was not a man who wanted to be found. But Jem and Merinda were determined, and soon they were in Corktown, following him up the street. Merinda tucked her walking stick under her arm and picked up her pace. Jem walked just at her heels. Without the restriction of skirts and stays they could easily cross the road and match his speed.

They caught up to him. "Stop, wait," Merinda said.

Fred flinched. "I have no time for—" He squinted at them under their bowler hats. "Hang on. You're a girl! And so are you!"

"You didn't kill Fiona," Merinda said.

He remained flummoxed. "I what? Yes! I mean, no! Of course not."

"I know you were taken in for questioning," Merinda said, "and I was there at the Elgin when...when Grace was killed."

Fred cocked his head to the side, suddenly interested in what she had to say. "There's a coffee house just up here past Massey Hall," he said.

Merinda and Jem followed him in, and they sat and ordered a pot of black coffee.

Fred twisted his tweed cap nervously in his calloused hands. "How do you know I didn't kill Fiona? I mean, I know I didn't, obviously. But the police aren't convinced, I fear."

Merinda sipped her coffee. "I think it unlikely that the man who was enraged enough to risk his freedom by barging into Montague's soirée waving a pistol would be the same man who carried off the murders of two young women. You were filled with grief, I think, Mr. O'Hare. Blinded by it, as your impassioned presence at the theatre demonstrated."

Fred stared ruefully into his coffee cup. "And what's it to you?"

"I'm investigating the Corktown murders for what they are," Merinda said.

Fred sat very still, and Jem feared he might be preparing to stand and flee. But he stayed put. "They kept me in holding overnight. But they couldn't find a motive or any evidence, so they let me out."

"The two girls were strangled," Merinda said as calmly as if she were discussing the weather.

He seemed to shrink. "Yes. Fee and I were engaged for a year. I was so close to saving enough."

"Did you suspect she was...familiar with any other men?"

The tips of Fred's ears flamed as red as his hair. He swallowed some of his anger with a long sip of coffee. "Of course not." His voice croaked. "But she did go out."

"She did?" Merinda leaned forward.

"Most Thursday evenings. To a dance hall on Elm Street. I went once or twice but I often worked the night shift. We were this close..." A single tear snaked down his cheek, and Jem's heart clutched at the sight. "This close," he repeated, looking between them, "to being able to afford a home of our own."

When they got back home, Merinda made a note of the Elm Street Dance Hall on the chalkboard in the sitting room.

Jem was just happy to recline by the fire and read a book, far away from danger and murder suspects. But the wheels in Merinda's head were turning at a rapid pace.

In the tea room at Spenser's Department Store the next day, as Jem enjoyed her break, a delivery boy she only knew in passing stared up at her with a gapped-tooth smile and asked, "Hey, Jem! Isn't this your friend? This Merinda Herringford girl?"

"Yes, why?"

"You're two steps from famous. Think I'll hire you to find that fiver I lost on the shop floor last week."

He handed her copy of the *Hog*. On the society and arts page was a small boxed advertisement:

> Mystery or theft? No problem too big or too small for two lady detectives. Apply Herringford and Watts, 395 King St. West. Consultations and deductions for a reasonable fee.

Jem's jaw dropped. All of Toronto had her address. She flung the *Hog* away and spent the rest of her shift plotting how best to ream her lodgemate out when she returned home. When Tippy returned from her own tea break, she could barely suppress the laughter teasing the corners of her mouth and lighting her eyes.

Tippy smiled broadly. "You're a detective!"

"I am not!" Jem was adamant, and she dashed out as soon as she possibly could and sprinted to the nearest streetcar.

When she reached their flat, she saw a bold sign hanging in the front window: *Herringford and Watts: Lady Detectives for Consultation and Hire.*

Jem bounded into the sitting room, already imagining the riff-raff they'd collect from the street with such blatant advertisement. "Mer-in-*da!*"

"Jem! Isn't it wonderful? We're Sherlock and Watson."

"We are nothing of the sort." Jem tossed her coat at the longsuffer-ing Mrs. Malone and wagged her finger at Merinda. "You can Sher-lock all you want. I am starving and tired and I want to rip up that sign before half of the city is on our doorstep. How did you get the *Hog* to run the ad so quickly?"

"I paid DeLuca extra. Also, we really do need to give that fellow his coat and book and watch back."

Jem flushed a little.

"He was so polite about it," Merinda continued. "Gentlemanly enough to—listen to this—refer to you as nothing more than the odd hobo girl on the steps of the benefit." She giggled. "Imagine his keep-ing that indiscretion to himself. The man I know from those muck-raking pieces on the Don Jail would have hung you out to dry if it meant earning a few more pennies from the newsies on the Queen beat."

"You talked to him?"

"I bartered. And here we are. An advertisement for our exciting new venture. A business! We'll start with the Corktown Murderer and then move to the top."

"What did you give him in exchange?"

"The promise of his coat," Merinda smirked. "Take his things by the *Hog* offices tomorrow, will you?"

By eight thirty that evening, it seemed that half the city was stand-ing on their doorstep or chattering in their foyer. Jem helped Mrs. Malone move chairs from every corner of the house, and she and Mer-inda received their clients one at a time in the sitting room.

"Why does no one ask our qualifications?" Jem broke into one girl's soliloquy about a priceless family heirloom pilfered from her purse as she took it to the jewelers for appraisal. "Miss...Tremblant was it?"

"H-Harriet Tremblant."

"Yes. Well, we are not qualified." Jem thrust a finger in Merinda's direction. "*She* is not qualified."

"H-how much do you charge?"

"For you? A first-time client?" Merinda was near bouncing out of her seat. "It's positively free!"

Harriet Tremblant clapped her hands.

By the end of the night, they had fifteen open cases. No one cared a smidge about credentials. They were lady detectives, after all, who could be trusted to handle delicate matters. When it came down to it, and despite all her reservations, Jem simply didn't have the heart to turn these girls away. Many of them came straight from the Ward, burdened with problems that pressed down their shoulders. Merinda had been right: The *Hog* did reach the widest number of readers. It was a rag, yes, and a cheap one at that. Two pennies cheaper than the *Globe and Mail* or the *Daily Telegraph*. But advertising with them was effective.

As the last girl was escorted out, Merinda gave a triumphant little dance. Jem still hadn't had any supper and her head positively ached from hunger. Her temper, too, had worn thin.

"Finally, something exciting!" Merinda yawned. "Don't forget to give DeLuca back his coat and notebook and watch tomorrow."*

"Merinda," Jem said, "you cannot possibly think that we can help these girls. They trust us. We are not qualified."

"Your parents cut you off," Merinda said. "What else do you have to do with your time?"

"Gainful employment!"

"We have on more than one occasion given aid to the Toronto Constabulary."

"You have trailed Jasper Forth like a puppy dog, is more like it. And now look what's happened to the poor man."

"Can't you just see the headlines? 'Herringford and Watts stomp out the Morality Squad!'"

---

* Merinda Herringford's deductive powers failed to stretch far enough to recognize the possibility that while Jem had every intention of returning Ray DeLuca's watch and coat, the journal had winnowed its way into her heart and was worth far more to her than a few interesting notes from his muckraking stint in the Don Jail.

Jem threw up her hands. "'Herringford and Watts get thrown in jail!'"

"'Herringford and Watts become Toronto's premiere investigators!'"

"Herringford and Watts better get fed soon or Watts won't be long for their new enterprise."

Merinda stuck her tongue out. Jem stuck out hers in answer. Still, despite herself, Jem couldn't help but grin.

Toronto had no idea what it was in for.

CHAPTER FIVE

Toronto is an endless maze. Even its most adventurous
citizen may never completely unravel every one of
its corners and nooks. I try, as any intrepid reporter
might, to follow the heartbeat of the city. But where
does that heartbeat lie? In St. John's Ward, with the
newly arrived immigrants exhausted from their
journey and terrified of what they might find in
their new, safe start? In City Hall, where Horace
Milbrook works through the mire of corruption
to exact some kind of good and social promise?

An excerpt from a journal Jem is not supposed to be reading

Ray DeLuca had many wonderful qualities: his loyalty to his family; his quick mind, which allowed him to soak up English and make it his second language; his smile, which, when fully stretched across his face, could force clocks to stop and crocuses to bloom; and his unwavering passion for societal reform.

His temper, on the other hand...

Ray dashed around the circumference of the small room with the air of a perturbed fox. He'd spent the night at Vi's place again, after stopping to bring her dinner and discovering Tony, once again, missing. He couldn't be there all the time, but he would be there as often as he could.

Viola's eyes narrowed at him as she hoisted young Luca higher on her hip. "What's got you so agitated?"

Ray exhaled. He went to the old basin and splashed ice-cold water on his face. At least he felt awake. It was when he caught his reflection in the mirror that it hit him: *St. Joseph's!* He had left his hat there to reserve his space in the crowded bunkroom. There was a sort of collective trust at the house, so he figured it would still be sitting there when he returned. He exhaled.

"Ray?"

"Yes, Viola?"

"You'll see again about a job for Tony?"

Beautiful Viola with her black hair and dark circles around her eyes. In the daylight, he saw bruises that had been cloaked by the darkness of the night before. He took in the absent way her long fingers wound themselves in Luca's small sprout of curls. Beautiful Viola, whom the morning light had once courted so well. Beautiful Viola and her horrid taste in men.

"I'll try, Vi."

Find Tony a job. If only it were that easy. Ray had played this game before. The first step was always finding Tony at all. The next steps were to convince him to come home to his wife and baby and to not buy liquor with every last penny he made at the roundhouse or the brickworks. Then Ray would have to convince Tony to stop yelling and stop hitting and...

He grabbed an apple from a chipped bowl on their small table and tossed it up and down. *"Ciao, mio piccolo anatracoccolo."* Goodbye, my little duckling. It was what Ray had called Viola since they were children. He kissed her on the cheek and mussed Luca's hair before stepping, coatless, into the September air.

The autumn breeze and the early morning sun drained the last of his frustration. As it did every day, the city talked to him in all the languages of the world. He loved its vivacity and vibrancy, the unending music of footfalls, of trolleys on tracks, of the horses' hooves. He loved hearing the merchants hawking their wares from one side of the bustling street to the other.

As he sloped southward to the harbor, the glistening lake caught the kiss of the sun, and he tuned his ears for the bellow of the ships' arrivals. Ray could imagine the girls in pigtails and the boys playing with yo-yos way back in third class, their parents in overworn outer clothes, threadbare and not warm enough to see them through the onslaught of winter. He could see all of them inching their way toward a new life.

Ray still believed in this new life. Despite the prejudice waiting for all immigrants—including himself—at every corner. Despite the meetings in the back of the new City Hall claiming Canada for Canadians. He believed in it as his mother had, though she had not survived the sea voyage. And he would make the most of her memory, even if it meant continually putting Viola's needs ahead of any chance he could have for a personal life.

"You need to get out more, Mr. DeLuca," Skip McCoy told him daily. "You're not a bad-looking guy. Some girls will swoon for that accent of yours. They like all the poetic Italian stuff. Go to the dance halls. There's one on Elm Street. I'll take you. Dance a little. *Live* a little. Right now, your primary relationship is the *Hog,* and believe me, it's not worth it. She'll never love you back."

Ray did as he usually did when Skip had one of these moments: He avoided his eyes and shuffled papers around on his desk and bellowed for another typewriter ribbon.

"I've a nice girl for you." Even McCormick, the *Hog's* editor, was willing to step up. "You gotta watch that temper of yours and your odd ways, DeLuca. But I know someone from my wife's knitting circle who hires a seamstress. Cute. Catholic girl. You're a little on the short side, but my wife says if you smile more often—full-on smile—the ladies will line up around the block for a glimpse of you. I wouldn't know anything of this kind of stuff myself, mind you. But she says—"

Ray had raised his hand to stop him. His purpose was not to find personal happiness but to keep his sister and nephew's heads above water. He was fortunate enough to do this while scratching out a living as a second-rate hyperbolic wordsmith. At least the job required words. Ray couldn't live if not by words.

Ray strolled across the red brick road to a warehouse overrun with old printing presses and the smell of ink, ambition, and sweat. These were the crude offices of the *Hogtown Herald*. He made for the tiny lean-to off the furnace room, where his overturned-crate-for-a-chair and table waited. The tabletop was slanted, ink-spotted, and scarred from years of use. His office.

Ray dipped the nib of his pen in a small pot, and the first of the day's many black spots splattered on his hand. He wondered when Miss Watts would come by with his belongings. Merinda Herringford had promised the return of his coat in exchange for the prompt placement of her advertisement.

Certainly the girl wouldn't have had the audacity to go through his coat pockets, would she? Certainly she wouldn't find his journal—and read it. Or *would* she? He already knew she had the nerve to plant herself, broad and brash as can be, under a streetlight clad as a man. She'd pulled off the disguise fairly well, right up until the moment when her drawers had dropped. She certainly hadn't looked like a man in that split second before he'd turned away.

A few hours later, Ray had crafted an editorial piece on Montague's rally and the second corpse that he thought was a cut above the usual muckraking drivel he was known for. *Suspected murderer and mayor, Montague shrouded in secrecy and death.* Ray was inspired, typing swiftly, until he couldn't tell where his fingers left off and the keys of his Underwood began. He was lost in thought when Skip knocked at the wooden beam framing his cubby.

"A young lady to see you, Mr. DeLuca." His voice was formal. He leaned into Ray's ear. "A very attractive young lady."

Ray turned around in surprise and found himself facing a beautiful woman, well-dressed and looking at him with bright eyes and a rather flushed face. When their eyes met, Ray blinked several times. This was the awkward and squeaky girl from the other evening? Surely not, for this was no girl. If ever a figure was worthy of the word *woman,* it was she.

"Thank you very much for loaning me your coat." She handed him his coat, her cheeks deep red. Doubtless she was playing over the last time they had met.

"You're very welcome, Miss Watts." He studied her face. "I didn't recognize you."

She studied him right back. "You're staring at me."

Ray raised an eyebrow. "You're staring at *me.*"

"Sorry," she said as a dimple appeared on her right cheek. She was so very pretty. Innocently pretty. Fresh-faced pretty.

He laughed, surprised. "You'll pardon me, but on our previous meeting I didn't see that you were so beautiful."

Her cheeks flushed deeper red. "Thank you for running our ad," she said.

"Yes, of course. Anything to get my coat back." He laughed while noticing her proper, corseted curves and fashionable daysuit. "At least now I know why you were there last night. A lady investigator!" He patted the coat. "Did you happen to find anything in the pocket? When you were"—he held up his sleeve and searched for a phrase—"making my coat smell like flowers?"

Jem smiled and looked away briefly. "Mrs. Malone—my house-keeper—laundered and pressed it. I hope you don't mind. The smell. It's lavender. It's my favorite and..." She broke off. Ducked her head. "What was in the pocket?"

"My notebook. A diary of sorts."

"Mrs. Malone would've emptied the pockets before laundering."

"Of-of course." he said, a quick response while the severity of the loss hit him. It couldn't cover what he felt at the sudden loss of words gone forever. His last day in Italy. His first day in Toronto. The sights and smells. The slow, arduous task of learning English. He exhaled and ran his hand over his face. Abominable luck. At least...yes, the pocket watch was still there. "Thank you," he said heavily.

She smiled at him again. Gave him another long look and turned toward the door.

"Wait! Wait a moment!" He liked the way the light played off her high cheekbones when she turned her head over her shoulder. "I want my interview. How did a woman like you end up a lady investigator?"

"All women have secrets, Mr. DeLuca."

Ray began to think in poetry.* This Jemima Watts, she was soft. Her curls were milk chocolate. Her eyes were the persistent kiss of waves on the shore at dusk, their light like sun spilling over water. He loved the way she wrinkled her nose, the way her smile tugged into a solitary dimple in her right cheek.

"You're staring at me again," said Jem.

"Well, yes," he said. "I hadn't noticed the other night that you were so beautiful. And now I am forced to wonder about my reporter's powers of observation."

"Mr. DeLuca, you're a good flatterer."

"Believe me, I'm not trying."

"He's not." Ray had forgotten that Skip existed until he spoke. "He doesn't flatter."

Ray growled. "Go back to your typesetting!† *Fretta!*"

Skip laughed.

Jem wrinkled her nose. "I should go."

"It's been a pleasure, Miss Watts."

He hugged his coat to his chest and brought the sleeve to his nose. Lavender.

---

* Ray's poetry was terrible. A strange hybrid of Wordsworth and Tennyson that went on at length about nature.

† The *Hogtown Herald* was skeletally staffed. Skip was a bit of a genius jack-of-all-trades who picked things up rather quickly. Since Ray had met him he had easily been able to work his way around a press as well as take and process all of their photographs. When Ray asked, impressed, where he had picked up so many skills, Skip always replied, "Oh, here and there" with a shrug.

The Ward was a maze, and Jem and Merinda's goals of finding lost items or reuniting mothers with their truant offspring were daunting. But at least, Jem decided, their recent days had been free of corpses. She still hadn't shaken the sight of the statue-still woman splayed on the carpet of the Elgin Theatre.

The *Globe and Mail* and the *Daily Telegraph* had stopped running pieces on the Corktown Murders. The *Star* and the other dailies were focused on politics and the new idea for a subway train station. The newsies outside Spenser's were raising a cacophony about the rising rate of immigration in the Ward, rampant crime, and Tertius Montague's new laws regarding females.

Merinda seemed immune to the news around her. Instead, she was elated at their new enterprise. When she wasn't carefully studying her Sherlock Holmes stories she was rereading M.C. Wheaton's *Guide to the Criminal and Commonplace*—frequently quoting whole pages of it at a time whenever Jem returned from her shift. She'd also commissioned a carpenter to make a larger *Herringford and Watts: Lady Detectives* sign for the doorway. But they were far from household names, except in the Ward, where their pro bono service was on the lips of every lady in a predicament.

Business was steady,* so Jem balanced her shifts at Spenser's with her need to dash home to aid Merinda. Tippy was generally so preoccupied with the packages that Jem could slip away unnoticed before the five o'clock bell.

The trunk coughed up a deerstalker. Somehow Merinda had acquired a Toronto police uniform of a size much smaller than would fit Jasper, and it came into play as well.

"And look!" Merinda made her newly printed calling cards rain down on the Persian carpet. "We are authentic detectives. I have schooled Mrs. Malone in proper client protocol. She will lead the client into the sitting room to wait. We'll put magazines and leaflets there. Then we'll receive our clients just like Holmes and Watson."

---

* If non-paying investigations could be called business.

Merinda was no Holmes and Jem was no Watson, but that didn't keep them from trying. They found lost items and reunited cousins. They learned that Susan's husband had gambled away their savings, that Drusilla had a long-lost brother named Frank, and that Anne had tricked Martha to get a better job. They discovered that Freida had sabotaged Esther's workstation, and they returned little Tommy to his mother's eager arms. They bandied with suffragettes and parleyed with petty thieves.

They got little sleep and made no money whatsoever. But they learned, through it all, that they possessed genuine talent as a sleuthing team. Merinda had a natural knack for deduction and Jem had a way of placating Merinda, of putting their clients at ease, and of acting as an intermediary as Merinda bounded around with poor manners. She was so far beyond the conventions of proper female behavior that bystanders were downright appalled—until they found themselves thanking the girls for work done on their behalf.

But no matter how busy they got, neither Jem nor Merinda could shake the image of the two dead girls, nor the photographs of the mourning families that Ray DeLuca had run in the *Hog*.

Ray DeLuca, indeed, seemed the only remaining way to glean any information, not only on the Corktown Murders, but also on the plight of women pursued by Mayor Montague's indefatigable Morality Squad. While the other papers preferred to trumpet Montague's benevolence, DeLuca and his paper seemed more carefully attuned to what was happening on the periphery. Montague's band was cracking down harder than ever on enforcing laws curtailing women's freedoms. Women were warned not to set foot alone on the city streets as the sun ducked away and autumn drew colder.

Merinda was particularly keen on observing the bylines of one Gavin Crawley, star reporter at the *Globe* and one of the Morality Squad's most vocal advocates. Crawley was a striking contrast to DeLuca. His paper was conservative, well-respected, and, to many Torontonians, the only one worth consulting. But it turned Merinda's stomach to read his diatribes on "female incorrigibility" and his ongoing belief that unmarried women were filtering into the city to entice respectable men.

Merinda and Jem knew from their investigations in the Ward that these sentiments were making conditions difficult on honest workingwomen. How could they stay indoors after dark when night fell before they were released from their shifts? How could they get home without a cloud of suspicion falling on them for being out at night? Many walked together in huddled groups, looking around like agitated bunnies as they skittered to streetcars or dashed across streets to reach their homes.

Such were Jem's musings as she walked home from Spenser's one evening. The days were growing colder, and it was with a sense of relief that she found herself back at King Street. She hung up her coat and scarf and retreated to the sitting room, where Merinda sat with a fresh pot of tea—and Tippy.

"Tippy?" said Jem, brushing the snowflakes out of her hair. "I didn't know you were coming for dinner tonight. Why didn't you tell me? We could have walked together."

Merinda was all business. "Jem, Tippy tells me that her sister, Brigid, might know something about the Corktown Murders."

Jem stared. That someone she'd worked beside for so long might have a connection with those murders was upsetting. "Tippy? Is this true?"

Tippy shrugged shyly. "Brigid's been getting strange notes from an anonymous source. And I...well, I worry that she might be the next target."

"Why didn't you tell me at work?" Jem asked, sharing a look with Merinda.

"I was scared. I didn't know what to do. But when I saw your ad..." Tippy trembled. "Well, I thought maybe you could help."

Merinda stood and paced in front of the fire. "You knew Fiona and Grace," Merinda murmured thoughtfully.

"We all lived in the same boardinghouse. And Grace worked with my sister. With Brigid."

"Where?"

"The King Edward hotel. In the laundry." Tippy reached into her handbag and extracted a sheet of paper. Upon it were several threats, formed in cut-and-paste fashion from what appeared to be an assortment of periodicals.

"How curious!" Merinda exclaimed.

"I want them to stop," Tippy said. "Brigid's scared. I'm scared. Whoever is sending these knows where we work and where we live." A tear pricked her green eye and started a slow descent down her pale, freckled cheek.

Jem offered Tippy a handkerchief. "Now, now, you've come to the right place. We'll get this all sorted."

Merinda growled. "Stop your sniveling, Tippy. And Jem, stop encouraging her! Take your handkerchief back! Now, Tippy, how many letters has your sister received?"

"A dozen," Tippy said. "This is the most recent one, but here: I've brought them all." She extracted a small stack of letters from her bag.

Merinda's nose scrunched up as she read. The notes spoke to Brigid's close relationship with Fiona and Grace and warned her to keep her mouth shut, not to ask any questions.

"She always receives them at work?" Merinda asked.

"Just before the end of the day."

Merinda smiled. "I know *exactly* what to do."

Shortly thereafter, Mrs. Malone escorted Tippy out and Merinda paced again before throwing herself in her chair in front of the fire, pressing her fingers to her temples. "I think we have finally been hired to solve the Corktown Murders!" she said elatedly. "And it's about time."

"Is that what you've been hoping for?" Jem asked. "I still don't think we're experienced enough for that case."

Merinda wasn't listening. "When you have eliminated the impossible," she said, chewing her lip, "whatever is left, however improbable..."

"Must be the truth."

CHAPTER SIX

*One cannot expect that everything will be tied up
in a neat knot. Life's greater mysteries and the turn
of fortune's wheel work outside the realm of human
ability. Try to succeed, but allow yourself moments
of weakness. Focus on the art of acceptance when it
doesn't all come together in the way you had planned.*

Guide to the Criminal and Commonplace, M.C. Wheaton

DeLuca!" McCormick was a bass drum as he entered the office. The rotund, owl-faced editor threw his coat on his desk, his face stormy.

Ray reclined in his chair, chewing the end of his pencil. "Sir?"

"The state of the *Hog*!"

Was it a question or a statement? "The state of the *Hog*...is good?"

"That's the answer I pay you for?"

"That and my penny-dreadful rehashing of popular events."

"I'm tired of this Corktown Murder story. We need something like the Don Jail piece. If we don't get it, the *Hog* goes under. As soon as you blink you'll be back where I found you—hunched over, two years away from rheumatoid arthritis, digging railway tunnels near the Roundhouse."

Ray was unfazed. "The Corktown Murders are important. And as of yet unsolved. Montague's theatre. Montague's maid."

"People have forgotten those stories, man. The *Hog* is the only paper still splashing them about." McCormick barreled forward.

"We're becoming a laughingstock. Believe it or not, I still strive toward respectability."

"I know. And that's why it's important we continue to follow the story. It sets us apart."

"*Too* far apart. People think we're crazy. Still chasing after threads. You never lay off Montague. And people are complaining."

Ray leaned forward with interest. "Who is complaining?"

"Chief Tipton, for one. He has asked me to desist. As has the Toronto Council. They have threatened to shut us down."

Ray blinked. Then blinked again. "For speculating? For reminding people of the little evidence we have on these unsolved murders?"

"It's giving Montague a bad name, this 'speculation,' as you call it. It's hitting too close to home, I wager, and he has powerful allies. Do you want to come in here one morning and find our printing presses at the bottom of Lake Ontario?"

"Of course not." Ray ran a hand through his hair. "But we've invested a lot in this story."

"And Montague has invested a lot in his Morality Squad," said McCormick. "Lay off the women's thing."

"The *women's thing*?" Ray was incredulous. "These families never see their daughters again, McCormick. What if it was my sister?"

"This isn't about you, DeLuca."

"Sir, you hired me because I was the only one willing to get into the mire of the city and exhume its dirt. Well, that's what I am doing, still, when no one else will."

"Fine. Well done. And now I need an article that won't step on people's toes," said McCormick. He removed his glasses and wiped the lenses on his shirt. "We lay off Montague for a while and we get back in his good books. That's why you're going to go see what's going on in that housing project of his in the Ward. St. Joseph's, I think it's called."

Ray smirked. "Ten steps ahead of you. Moved in already. St. Joseph's is a flophouse."

The side of McCormick's mouth threatened to tilt into an approving smile, but he quickly ironed it out. "It's a workingmen's hotel."

McCormick coughed, not meeting Ray's gaze. "Montague's made affordable housing a priority, and we're going to applaud him for it. Just get it done, will you?"

Ray didn't bother to respond as McCormick walked away. He slumped on his slat of a desk and rubbed his temples. An investigative piece that Montague wouldn't find irksome. Should he try to paint St. Joseph's as something other than the flophouse that he knew, from his own time there, it actually was?

Blinking his bleary eyes into focus, he noticed an advertisement mock-up on the side of his desk. It was the advert for Herringford and Watts. The smell of lavender leaped to his mind, though his coat was across the room.

Ray became more curious about those ladies the more he heard about them. And heard about them he had. Just last week, as he'd crossed from Viola's cottage back to University Avenue, he'd overheard an exchange between ladies hanging out their laundry near the open water well in the Ward.

"They don't charge nearly as much as the man my husband mentioned," one had chirped.

"Sometimes they don't charge at all!" said another.

Ray had inched closer, removing his hat.

"That can't be," said a woman bouncing a baby on her hip.

"Lucy got their card from Mary, who got it from one of the girls at the shirtwaist factory!"

"Women belong in the home," said a woman with a sour voice, "not galloping around Toronto in pants! Sticking their noses where only the police should be."

"The police can't help! Ah, but women have intuition! They can understand and sympathize. I don't want some police detective investigating my private business."

"The tall blonde one canvasses at Simcoe Street," a woman said conspiratorially. "Makes sure that if you step off the train, you leave with all of your possessions. Last week, they found that one of the track workers was pocketing goods from the luggage compartments.

She caught him, gave him a piece of her mind, and dragged him over to a traffic cop."

This anecdote in particular had coaxed a smile up the side of Ray's face.

"The handsome traffic cop," added another. "The one on the King beat!"

The stories had trickled and tripped over each other. Now, snapped out of his memories, Ray turned the advertisement over in his fingers. McCormick wanted a new story? Fine. He was going to make those bachelor girls the talk of Toronto.

CHAPTER SEVEN

*Detective work brings out the best and worst of
every person, place, and thing one can imagine.
An opulent building may be exposed as a den of
iniquity. Beneath the elegant façade of a wealthy
aristocrat may beat the black heart of a killer.*

Guide to the Criminal and Commonplace, M.C. Wheaton

Cracker jacks, Jem, this will be a cakewalk!"*

The girls were on their way to the King Edward Hotel,
where they intended to pay Brigid a visit. Merinda fastened
a small magnifying glass to the front pocket of her shirtwaist as Jem
noted the wonders Mrs. Malone had worked on her previously over-
large trousers. As Merinda donned a tweed jacket and grabbed a
walking stick that doubled as a sort of crowbar, Jem decided that
rubber-soled ankle boots were far preferable to the fashionable heels
she had to wear at Spenser's.

There was no threat of rain that night, so they walked—two men,
or so they seemed—in companionable silence to the opulent hotel.

Merinda whistled as they neared Yonge on the west side of the
hotel. The King Edward took up half a block. The grand establishment was a fixed point in the kaleidoscope of the city.

"We'll sneak in the back," Merinda told Jem as they arrived and
stared up at the big blue banners, Union Jack flags, and awnings

---

* The astute reader will observe that when Merinda Herringford claims an adventure will be a
cakewalk, it rarely turns out to be so.

announcing, in gold monogrammed glory, the regal respectability of the place. "Head straight to the basement and the laundry. And if anyone asks, we're lost tourists."

The security guard at the back entrance was flirting with a scullery maid and didn't see them creep by. A few bare light bulbs dangled from solitary cords. The smell of bleach was almost tangible. Perspiration pricked the backs of their bare necks, hair tucked safely into their bowlers. They heard the gentle hums, ticks, and clicks of the under-wirings of the hotel.

The laundry room was cramped and its smell almost unbearable. Frowning women strained over great vats, their backs hunched and their muscles straining. Merinda and Jem shuddered.

The oldest woman stepped forward. "Who are you? How did you get down here?" The rest of the workers, at a stern glance from the forewoman, resumed stirring the large, misty pots, focusing with tired eyes.

"Your security was otherwise engaged," Merinda said.

"You can't be down here." She was a robust woman with coarse red skin. She planted her fists on her hips while narrowing her beady eyes.

"My name is Merinda Herringford, and this is my associate, Jemima Watts. We are here on behalf of a client."

The forewoman thrust her face toward them. "You're women!" A wave of babble and laughter rippled among the other workers, but she ignored them. "What do you mean, a client?"

Merinda extracted a card and held it up. "We're consulting detectives."

The woman wiped her bulky hands on her apron and inspected it. "Can't read."

"'Merinda Herringford and Jemima Watts, detectives for consultation,'" Merinda recited.

"Are you really detectives?" The question came from a woman in the corner, chestnut hair tumbling from her cap.

"Yes, indeed."

"Who is your client?" asked the forewoman.

"I cannot divulge that information publicly," said Merinda regally.

"I think..." the girl said, but then she shot a sheepish look at the growling forewoman. "Please? I think I know what this is about."

"Oh, go ahead. Anything to get them out of my sight. You have five minutes." She clapped her meaty hands. "Girls, back to work!"

Jem and Merinda walked down the gray corridor in the company of the young woman.

"You're Brigid," said Jem. "Tippy's sister. You've been receiving the letters."

"Yes. Yes, I have. Tippy told you?"

"We work together," Jem said.

"Just like you worked with Grace Kennedy," Merinda put in. "Did you know her well?"

Brigid was silent.

"If you know anything about what happened to her..."

"I don't," said Brigid. "I swear I don't know a thing. I barely knew her. Just to say hello."

"Whoever's sending these letters seems to think otherwise," said Merinda. "Do you know why she was at Mayor Montague's fundraising party on the night she died? It wasn't, perhaps, the most usual place for a girl from the hotel laundry to turn up."

"Quiet," said Brigid. "Not here. We can't talk here. Can you meet me at my boardinghouse later? It's in Corktown. Just off Parliament Street. Sunday afternoon, perhaps?"

"Of course," said Jem, scrawling the address on the back of a card. "We'll talk then. And I promise we'll do our best to keep you safe."

"I can't pay you," Brigid said. "There's nothing extra after the bit I send home to my dad."

"We won't worry about that," Merinda said kindly, and they deposited her back at the laundry and waved goodnight.

Merinda and Jem wound their way through the corridor, back the way they'd come. They were nearly at the door when Jem grabbed her friend's wrist. They stilled in the darkness.

Something was moving with them.

"It's probably just some night janitor or a rat," Merinda said, marching bravely on.

Jem stopped her again. "The footfall matches ours!" she whispered frantically.

They breathed a sigh of relief as they approached the exit, speedily sprinting up the stairs, shouldering the heavily metal door and exhaling in the night air.

A few steps on the pavement and Jem's senses were again pricked with the eerie suspicion that they were being followed. She whipped her head over her shoulder, but the noise and the whisper of a shadow that tickled the hairs at the back of her head had vanished.

They crossed the bustling traffic at Yonge and headed home, accustomed to the sound of horses neighing and trolleys skidding on tracks. A few reckless automobiles swerved under the bright electric marquees.

But Jem couldn't shake the feeling that the city was watching them.

CHAPTER EIGHT

*The first guide to honing your deductive skills is to
let the world fall away. You should be trained, like
a bloodhound on the scent, to keep your eyes on
the prize and allow nothing in your periphery.*

Guide to the Criminal and Commonplace, M.C. Wheaton

Playing bachelor girl detective, Jem decided as she gathered up
her things and prepared to head home, would be the last nail
in the coffin of her romantic prospects. The closest she'd come
to a man had been the many hours she'd spent reading Ray's journal. Any hope she might have had for personal happiness was buried
under bowler hats and scuffed boots.

As she hurried homeward, she became aware of a shadow behind
her. Ah, her familiar follower. Ever since the night at the King Edward,
she had felt this person's presence everywhere. Something Merinda
had said pricked the back of her mind. *There's a moment that hovers
between fear and frustration.*

She was in that moment now, and shadows appeared everywhere.

Jem tried to shrug the feeling off. Her light heels tripped over
the cracks in the roughly paved street, and she made out the sound
of a footfall in rhythm with her own. She sped up, and the pursuer
matched her pace. She slowed down, and its cadence softened behind
her.

She swooped up her skirts and made a hasty diagonal for the other
side of the street, barely avoiding the path of a raging automobile. In

a storefront window, she spotted a male figure, black in the falling dusk, crossing as well.

The Morality Squad. She might have known.

Jem straightened her shoulders and slowed her pace. When the footfalls neared, she swung around and faced the figure straight on.

"Are you following me?" she demanded.

The man stopped on the curb, surprised. But he didn't speak, and his face was in shadow.

"Look," Jem said, "I'm just off work and not far from home. It's not even six o'clock!" She made a quick assessment of her surroundings in case she needed to make a getaway. The streetlights hissed and flickered in the settling dark, a carriage's wheels spun in the near-frozen dirt a street over, and a few horses plodded by. Behind, on Yonge, the trolley lumbered noisily over the tracks. Familiar sounds all, but nonetheless she shivered, making her plan.

The figure stepped closer and, finally framed by light, Jem could make out his features. There was a cleft in his chin, his cheeks were finely etched, and he had silky blond hair perfectly trimmed. Jem wondered if she had seen him before.

"You're staring at me pretty intensely," he remarked.

"You were following me pretty closely," she retorted. Jem attempted to study his visage as Merinda would. Trying, vainly it would seem, to impress his image upon her mind, as she was learning to do from her companion. If his features alone were an open book, she could maybe play Holmes and surmise his occupation, circumstance, and background.

Oh, fiddlesticks! It wasn't working. She had seen, but, as Holmes chided Watson, she had not observed.

Meanwhile, his smile grew. "Quite finished?"

"Are you with the Morality Squad?"

He spread his hands innocently. "I mean no harm, Miss Watts. I was en route to your place of residence."

So he knew her name. And where she lived. "You have need of

our services?" She straightened her shoulders. They hadn't had a male client yet.*

"You could say that."

"And you are...?"

"Gavin Crawley. *Toronto Globe and Mail.*"

"The reporter?" She peered at him more closely. "That fellow with those bothersome tracts on women and morality?"

He bowed. "Among other things. And I want to interview Merinda Herringford."

"Miss Herringford granted you an interview?"

Gavin stepped back. "I confess, no. But I would like one."

"Good luck!" Jem spun on her heel and proceeded northward.

She could sense Gavin following. He was so close behind that his sleeve brushed hers.

"Miss Watts," he said as they walked, "I am interested in Merinda Herringford. I would like to do a story on her."

"She will not be interested."

"Please, if you'll hear me out." He pressed his hat to his chest entreatingly, and Jem stopped to face him. "Besides," he said, "I am doing you a courtesy. I sit on Montague's council for the Morality Squad."

"Aha!"

"Yes, but I am not *on* the squad. In any event, what you and Miss Herringford are supposedly doing, gallivanting around Toronto, purporting to solve these petty crimes...Well, some see that as little less than a criminal offense."

"Criminal! We've done nothing but help women who have no other place to turn."

"There, there. I know that you are an upstanding and virtuous young lady. You work at Spenser's, you come from good stock..."

"You seem to know a lot about me, Mr. Crawley."

---

* With the exception of one Mr. Murdoch and his lost chicken, Fidget. Merinda and Jem chose not to include this case in their official count.

"I am a reporter. This is my job."

She turned and strode toward home. "You're all milksop, high-ball rolling, money-making politician pleasers, is what you are."

They passed under another streetlight. The man was smirking. Smirking! "You don't hold back, do you?"

"Journalistic integrity dictates that one present the truth in the plainest fashion," Jem said. "We need not sugarcoat the underbelly of our city, as you do. Nor must we abandon our investigation into the callous murder of two young women."

"As opposed to the *Globe*?"

"The *Hog* still runs the Corktown piece," she said, feeling surprisingly defensive.

"Yes, and with nothing solid about it for weeks. Speculation and muckraking. That DeLuca writes nothing you should pay attention to. There are brains in that pretty little head of yours, Miss Watts, and you wouldn't want anything salacious in there besides."

Jem bit her lip. Something about the man's eyes, the way he walked, his voice even, interested her despite his condescension. But she didn't stop walking. "I'm sorry. I'm on edge these days, and I thought you were following me."

"Does that mean I can 'follow' you home?" His eyes twinkled in the moonlight. "Since we are both walking the same direction?"

Jem didn't reply, but nor did she stop him from walking in stride with her. Soon, they reached the townhouse and Jem motioned for Gavin to follow her up the stairs. Mrs. Malone, stunned that a man other than Jasper Forth had darkened the door, smiled and hurried off for the tea things.

They found Merinda lying on her stomach, in trousers, stockinged feet in the air as she flipped through the *Strand* magazine, no doubt in pursuit of a new detective story.

Jem cleared her throat loudly. "Mr. Gavin Crawley," she said, "may I present Miss Merinda Herringford."

Gavin bowed to Merinda, smiling and waiting for her to rise, as propriety dictated. But Merinda remained on the floor. She scowled, grunted, and mumbled something Jem was glad she couldn't hear.

Jem cleared her throat, inviting Gavin to sit in the armchair as she settled onto the sofa. Mrs. Malone arrived with the tea service, which featured assorted dainties arranged to ornament the tea. Jem pinched a fairy cake and licked the icing.

Merinda watched their guest with a clear look of annoyance. "Your tracts and your articles..." She shook her head and dramatically outstretched crossed wrists. "Scoop me up and take me to jail, Mr. Crawley. You probably have a long list of vagrant and indecent offenses I have committed."

"No doubt," he said with one raised eyebrow. "However, I'm not here for that. You interest me as a reporter." He looked between the two of them. "I would like to interview you for the *Globe and Mail*."

"No," Merinda said.

"No?" Gavin sounded amused.

"Currently the only paper I give two cents about is the *Hog*," Merinda said adamantly. "*They* are still reporting on the Corktown Murders."

"Not every mystery can be solved, Miss Herringford. That DeLuca fellow is all about raking the mire for speculation. No doubt it gains the *Hog* a few extra sales of their rag. The *Globe* is a little more legitimate than that."

Merinda chuckled. "The *Globe* rarely reports on anything but its perception of female inadequacy and boring politics. If I grant you an interview, you will no doubt mock our endeavors."

"That's a little unfair, Miss Herringford."

"Explain your sudden interest in trouser-wearing lady detectives, Mr. Crawley."

Gavin straightened. "I want to make the city safer for women. Clean up the streets. Surely you approve of such a goal. The Morality Squad does women a favor by separating the wheat from the chaff."

"As if a mob could do anyone a favor."

Gavin smiled and set his teacup on the tray. "I see you are decided, madam. I shall take my leave then."

"No," Merinda said, "it is I who shall be leaving." She stomped off upstairs—with an unnecessary theatricality.

This left Jem, hands folded in her lap, trying to scrape up some propriety. No matter who this man was or what he said, Jem fell back on her upbringing. He was their guest and deserved a polite reception. "Well…" she said, hoping to break the tension.

"I'm very sorry," Crawley said.

Jem was suddenly aware of the way the firelight played across his strong features. He could have been a magazine ad man with a tennis racket slung over his shoulder, sporting the latest boating shoes and a straw hat. "Don't be, Mr. Crawley. I suppose I have no right to ask this, but is there anything I can say to get you to refrain from printing Merinda's behavior in the *Globe*? I can see the headline now: *Belligerent Lady Detectives Scoff Gentleman Reporter*."

"Actually, Miss Watts," Crawley said, his smile widening, "there is something you can say."

"Oh, do tell!"

"Say you'll join me for dinner on Thursday evening."

M.C. Wheaton said that one must always prepare for an unanticipated turn of events. This was one rapid turn, Jem thought, even as she blushed and accepted the invitation.

❧

Thursday evening came, and Jem approved of Gavin's pleated pinstripes and brushed bowler, the fresh carnation in his buttonhole, and the shine of his spats. She could tell by the line of his suit and his attention to collar and crease that he was a step ahead of the men's department at Spenser's. He looked good on her arm, with his height and his broad rower's shoulders.

The conversation, on the other hand, was like the engine on one of those propeller boats. It started and sputtered, started again, and came to a screeching halt before hiccupping into a decent pace.

Probably that was her fault, Jem thought. Such a well-known personality as Gavin could hardly fail to be a sparkling conversationalist. Probably he would never want to see her again.

But on Sunday morning, Gavin attended St. James with her.

"Come with me," Jem pleaded to Merinda as she pulled her gloves over her wrists. "He'll be here in a moment, and people will talk if they see me walk in alone with him. There'll be all sorts of gossip."

But Merinda just gave a heavy sigh and repeated what she'd said many times before: God was a mystery she didn't particularly care to solve, and while Jem might be interested in seeing through a glass darkly, she preferred to grapple with *facts*. "Besides," she reminded Jem, "we're meeting Brigid after lunch, and I want time to look at those letters again before we do."

As Jem had expected, her entry into the sanctuary on Gavin's arm provoked a wave of hushed conversation throughout the pews. *You see, Mildred!* she imagined men saying to their wives. *That Watts girl isn't so strange after all!*

It must be confessed that with the *Globe and Mail's* star reporter sitting proudly next to her and the congregation whispering behind her, Jem heard very little of the sermon.

❧

On Sunday afternoon—delightfully devoid of Gavin, or so Merinda said—they disembarked the trolley at Trinity and strolled into the mouth of Corktown. Brigid's boardinghouse, when they presented themselves in front of it, was found to be rundown and gray—a damp old building that seemed to suck all the light from the air. As the afternoon was fine, Brigid suggested going for a walk rather than talking indoors.

"I worked for Montague for just a summer," Brigid explained as they strolled. "While I was there, Fiona started and she was so pretty and young and hopeful. She did me good."

"It must be very hard on you," Jem said, "all that has happened."

"My family thought someone must be intent on hurting girls from Corktown. You know, Fee and I liked to go out to the dances at Elm Street. We enjoyed ourselves. Maybe it was someone from there. Morality police and all that."

"The Morality Squad doesn't usually kill people," Jem said.

"And you're not reckless," Merinda added.

"No," Brigid insisted. "We never were. We stuck together and walked home together. We kept our arms covered and our skirts to regulation."

Merinda pursed her lips. "Was Fiona walking out with a young man?"

"I think she was. But she wouldn't tell me about him. At first, she was humming all the time and slipping off. It seemed like she'd found a good thing. But her mood changed and she became sad all the time. I asked her about this man and she said there was no one. One night...just before..." She broke off. "You know...*just before*..."

"Before she was murdered," Merinda said bluntly.

Brigid nodded. "Fee told me I should stop going to Elm Street dances. She'd met a man there and he wasn't who he said he was. He'd promised her everything. A new life and all that. But he was false. And then...And then she was gone."

They walked in silence a moment.

"You have no idea who this was?" Jem asked at length.

"Not a hint. I'd stopped working at Montague's by then and gotten the job at the King Edward laundry. And Fee...well..."

"What about these notes?" Merinda said.

"The notes tell me to keep quiet and to think before I speak." Brigid suddenly turned to look for danger in the crowd around them. Apparently seeing nothing troubling, she continued. "The notes all threaten that I'll be in trouble too. They keep mentioning Grace, who was a friend of mine. We worked together at the laundry, of course.

But I didn't know her as well as Fee." Brigid began to sniffle and Jem held out a handkerchief.

"When was the last time you received a note?" Merinda asked.

"Yesterday. I don't know what information I have that this person is so afraid I'll share. I have no..." She bit her lip. "I don't know if this is helpful, but one of the girls at the laundry recognized the man who brought the last note. His name is Forbes, and he is on the Morality Squad." She looked at Jem and Merinda. "Is that important?"

Jem shrugged. "It could be. Thank you."

Merinda looped her arm with Jem's as they strolled back home late that afternoon. "Isn't the city something?"

"It's something, all right." Jem wasn't as enamored with Toronto, especially with someone targeting young women. "Who's this Forbes fellow? Anyone you've heard of?"

"No," said Merinda. "But I certainly intend to find out."

CHAPTER NINE

*There is nothing so debilitating or hopeless as the
onslaught of winter in the Ward. As October collides
with November, the snow shrieks in. At first, it is
tantalizing: trails of dancing crystal that children
stick out their tongues to taste. But the flurries stir
heavily, the temperature plummets, and play is
suspended as they return to makeshift shelters that
do little to shield them from the elements. The Ward
groans as the cold deadens the skin and stabs the bone.*

Excerpt from a journal Jem still should not be reading

When Ray arrived at St. Joseph's it was as if the curtain of his
memory was pulled back and he was once more a young
man newly arrived in the city. He remembered how his
eyes were constantly rimmed blood-red and raw with dust and how
daylight and dusk blended into one unending day.

He remembered feeling hopeless, with coins too few—foreign
coins he had trouble learning to count. He remembered how certain he was that, because he couldn't understand the foreman, he was
being cheated of his full pay. He remembered how the rent was too
often due to their grim landlord, who seemed to be a wolf-man torn
from the pages of a fairy story.

When he began his exposé and prepared to face the flophouse
once more, Ray took a carpet bag so bare it was nearly worn through,
tossed in sweaters and trousers, socks and suspenders, a new notebook

(though he still longed for the old, comfortable one), and a ratty old Bible, a memento of the St. James poor box.

He ensured that the woodstove was off and the bed was made. He kept his sparse bookshelf dusted and the floor tidy. When addressed by others at the flophouse, he responded in gruff, one-word sentences. He kept cigarettes in his pocket and a flask by his bed. He'd use them to bribe a few friendships, especially if he felt someone could tell him about Montague and link him to the Corktown Murders. Yes, he was here for McCormick, but that didn't mean he couldn't keep his eyes open too.

If Montague wanted to restore the city to the "Toronto the Good" of old, Ray decided one morning while splashing frigid water on his face, surely he could begin by stocking his flophouse with something better than this, where mattress ticks overran the lice and where there was a sewage system a century more primitive than what he had left behind in his boardinghouse just a few blocks away.

The other occupants of the flophouse were an eclectic bunch. Lars, the Swede who kept the woodpile stocked, was silent but friendly. His height, girth, and broad shoulders assured no one crossed him. Then there was Forbes. He was more of a force than a man, making any room he entered immediately smaller.

On Ray's second night at St. Joe's, Forbes stood in the doorway, bellowing for volunteers. "I need men," he said with a slur.

Ray propped himself up on his elbow on his bed. "For what?"

"Does it matter?" Forbes said, glowering at Ray.

Ray cocked his head. "For pay?"

"Of course for pay."

Ray declined, but Forbes rustled up a few other takers. Ray watched out of the corner of his eye as they left the room, wondering if Tony was ever one of Forbes's volunteers.

He waited a moment, then hopped up, stepped into his shoes, and cracked open the window. The men around him, sleeping or nursing their flasks or cigars or shuffling through day-old newspapers, cared little that he might decide to follow their eager bunkmates into the cold night. Ray could just see Forbes and his volunteers passing under a streetlight. He grabbed his coat, tipped his hat to Lars, and set out after them.

Merinda had mystery on the brain constantly these days. It intruded into conversation every night at dinner and replaced her appetite. Mrs. Malone had prepared roast chicken, potatoes, and peas, and Jem ate them with relish after a day at Spenser's.

"Tippy's still staying late and fluttering about like an agitated bunny." Jem tore off a piece of roll. She enjoyed these moments, recounting to Merinda the moments of her day. "She's either in love or completely mad."

"There's no difference," Merinda said, taking a big bite of chicken. "You know," she said, nodding at Mrs. Malone's back, "if she wasn't such a good cook, I'd get rid of her."

"Merinda! She might hear you."

"What?" Her mouth was full again. "We don't need a chaperone, Jem. I want privacy. We could be latch-key girls."

"What's a latch-key girl?"

"No chaperones. No maids or check-ins. No breakfast if we don't want it. Free to leave our clothes wherever, come and go with whomever, without Mrs. Malone clucking her tongue in disapproval."

"Well," Jem said, lifting her water goblet, "your father would never allow that."

"My father's not here to give his primitive advice, is he?" Merinda picked at her dinner a little longer, then shoved back from the table and went into the sitting room. There, she ruminated aloud on her plan for the evening. "If Tertius Montague pays men to act as his personal street-cleaners until he wins this blasted election, then he could certainly hire men to take care of his business with girls he once employed! Maybe he didn't kill Fiona and Grace himself, but he could have orchestrated their murders."

"I'm still not sure what the motive would be," Jem said from the table.

"Maybe Fiona was the love of his life and he killed her in a moment of passion. But Grace saw it all, so he had to dispose of her too."

Jem laughed. "It's not like you to see the world so romantically."

"Let's find this fiend Forbes in his natural habitat, skulking around the Ward."

"Forbes?"

"Don't you remember?" Merinda asked. "Brigid told us about him. He's on the Morality Squad, and she said he brought one of those mysterious anonymous letters."

"Ah, yes," Jem said, reaching for another roll. "All right, first thing tomorrow."

"First thing tomorrow? Now, Jem, now! He probably frequents the Lion or one of those places on Elizabeth Street."

"We can't go there at night."

"The Corktown Murders aren't going to solve themselves."

"No. They will be solved by the police. By real detectives."

"Detectives like us!" Merinda clapped her hands. "To the trunk!"

Half an hour later, leaves danced around their heels in the street and the harvest moon allowed them to see as clearly as they might in daylight. Merinda, dressed in a too-large coat and trousers, rapped her walking stick against the pavement and whistled. Jem, also dressed as a man, shivered and looked about her, on edge.

The stench of sewage and whiskey mingled in the gutter beside them. Rats scurried for the shadows as Merinda and Jem sidestepped a mound of potato peels and rotting meat scraps from the butcher's. Through a distant window came the sound of a baby wailing, and they snuck past a patrol cop, tapping his stick on the ground and walking in time with the beat.

The constable changed direction and headed toward them. Intimidated by the revealing light of the streetlamp, Jem and Merinda ducked behind a low wall and waited.

From her vantage point, Jem took in St. John's Ward. Brick

structures and wooden shacks hugged each other, slanting toward the lake to the south. The north side was home to a few haberdasheries, a Jewish butcher's shop, and a grim tavern serving up watered whiskey and beer that had sat too long in oaken casks. The Lion.

The constable passed, and Merinda and Jem began walking again.

Merinda strolled, bold as brass, right to the front of the tavern. For her part, Jem gulped cold air and willed her stomach to desist its sudden flip-flops.

Merinda adjusted her bowler. "Ready?"

Jem shook her head. "No." But she'd never be ready, so she followed Merinda anyway.

"Don't say *anything*. If we're made out, we'll say we got lost on the way to a society meeting."

"Society of what?"

"Would you rather admit we're searching for the Corktown Murderer and Montague's thugs?"

"No."

"I thought not."

They went inside and had gotten no further than the doorway when a curtain of cheap tobacco rose over them. A few patrons glanced at them briefly as they arrived, but soon Merinda and Jem were invisible in the crowd. The clang of a tuneless piano gave a dissonant contrast to the raucous noise in the place. Sucked in, they meandered to the bar, Jem keeping tight on Merinda's heels.

It wasn't long before the name "Forbes" reached their ears, and they quickly located the man to whom it belonged. Forbes stood a foot taller than the men encircling him. He was giving instructions of a sort, and Jem and Merinda shifted along the sticky bar to better hear the conversation. He was promising the men money and decent work.

Merinda lowered her mouth to Jem's ear. "So that's Montague's Morality Squad."

"Mayor Montague is this close to winning the election and getting a second term," Forbes said. "Which would benefit us all, gents. The people want someone who puts ideas into action." He explained, poorly, Montague's dedication to returning Toronto's reputation to its Victorian morality. They even drank to "Toronto the Good."

A patron twice as large as Jem and with sour breath approached her. "Got a light?"

She exhaled and kept her mouth clenched shut, hoping Merinda would step in. But her friend was preoccupied watching Forbes and company in the corner. The stench of liquor was so tangible on the man she could taste it before it dissolved in salty bile at the back of her throat. She shook her head.

"You're not one for speaking," the man persisted.

Jem lowered her voice: "I-I'm waiting for someone."

The man positioned himself onto a barstool, but even so he was several inches taller than Jem, who remained standing. He squinted at her, then reached over and abruptly plucked the cap from her head. "You're a woman!"

Several onlookers gave Jem their sudden attention. Even Merinda whipped her head over her shoulder, concern flashing in her eyes. She gripped the walking stick at her side.

"I'm c-coming from a society meeting," Jem explained lamely.

Beefy knuckles gripped the plait of hair down Jem's back and pulled her close, and she gave a little shriek. "Forbes will know what to do with you."

Jem thought fast and hard. She looked to Merinda, who still hadn't been found out. Merinda mouthed one word to Jem: *Run.*

Jem spied the open door and swooped her cap from the counter. She yanked herself free from the large man and made quickly for the exit, spry and much faster than her pursuer with his lumbering stride. She ran and ran, hearing him cursing behind her. Rounding Center Street, she lost him.

She stood breathing hard in the shadows, hoping Merinda would follow soon.

Unattended dogs yelped on the soggy cement. The streets were mostly deserted at this time of night, but through windows she could hear babies screeching while nearly all the languages of the world chimed discordantly. Jem pulled her cap back on and tucked her hair deep into its folds, keeping her eyes down and remembering to walk with her legs and not her hips. She kept her gaze downward, focusing on the first sprinkling of snow on the street.

So, when she collided with someone so hard she had the wind knocked out of her, she could do little but gasp, waiting for her breathing to return to normal.

Muffled laughter met her ears.

"What's so funny?" she demanded.

"Perfect! I was hoping to run into you, and I did. Literally."

Jem's words fled. *That voice!* The one laced with chocolate and moonlight. She turned her gaze onto the dark hair and eyes she had sketched a thousand times in her head.

Ray DeLuca.

"Jemima Watts," he said, helping her up. "Posing as a man again, I see."

She brushed herself off and took her first full breath since the collision. "Are you here reporting something, Mr. DeLuca?"

"I might be reporting you. Who's to say I haven't followed the girl in trousers halfway around the city?"

"Reporting me? I—"

"Calm down." He led her to the side of the street. A group of revelers passed, moving in the direction of the Lion tavern, from which she'd just run.

Jem lowered her voice. "I haven't done anything wrong."

"Of course you haven't." Ray looked her over. "This is the second time I've found you wandering around at night wearing men's clothing. Silly girl." Ray shook his head.

"I am *not* silly."

He raised his eyebrow. "Really?"

"I am here on important business." The look he gave her stirred her wrath. "In fact, I am here on behalf of a client."

"A client?" His eyes flashed. "Who?"

"That information is confidential, Mr. DeLuca."

"This," he said, indicating her getup, "is very amusing but very dangerous. Where's the other one?"

"Just finishing up at the Lion."

Ray extracted his notebook and pencil. He knew he should be dashing over there, leaving Jem to keep Forbes and his recruits in sight, but he wasn't going to leave this girl out here in the middle of nowhere.

"Jem!" A loud whisper reached them.

"Ah." Ray couldn't keep irony from his voice. "The other one."

"Jem! Jem! You'll never believe...whoa!" Merinda stopped and looked at Ray. "*Hogwash Herald!* You're here too!" She rapped her crowbar stick in her open palm.

"Miss Herringford." He tipped his hat.

Merinda grabbed Jem's elbow and pulled her aside. "I found Forbes. I bought him a drink. He had a pair of snakes with him and—"

"And I was nearly assaulted back there!" Jem said breathlessly.

Ray's eyes widened at the exchange. "Assaulted?" He looked around. "By whom?"

"It doesn't matter," Jem said, still looking at Merinda. "I'm fine."

"I am glad I found you both." Ray put one hand on Merinda's shoulder and one hand on Jem's and turned them to face him. "I have a proposal for you, and I will make it while walking you both safely to the streetcar stop." He turned them both around and started marching.

"What's this proposal of yours?" asked Merinda.

"I'd like to make you two the subject of my next serial in the *Hog*. It will be an easy exchange," Ray promised, giving them one of his easy smiles—though, Jem noticed, not one that reached his eyes. "I will not report you to the authorities, and you will talk to me exclusively."

"Report us to the authorities?" Jem was flabbergasted. "You wouldn't!"

Ray shrugged so innocently Jem couldn't tell whether he was serious or not. "I thought you would be the type to go for a...what *is* the word...*ultimatum.*"

"I am *not* the type," Merinda said. "Neither is Jem."

"I can't help but be useful to you," Ray persisted. "The exposure is free advertisement for your business. Besides, I do you a courtesy by asking. If you were anyone else in the city, I would write without permission."

"Free advertisement." Merinda said, distractedly. "It would expand the business."

"Of course it could." Ray was adamant. "Everyone will read about you." Ray looked between the pair, a slight smile creeping up the side of his mouth. "I want to continue to write about the Corktown Murders, as well. So if you stumble upon anything... Though I *should* be telling you it is dangerous and not appropriate for women and you would be better off darning socks or joining a ladies' society!"

Merinda's eyes under the streetlight were pure green fire: "Will you undermine us... as *girls*?"

"I am sure the two of you are·likely to do anything you decide to do."

Merinda gave him a Cheshire grin, and Ray took it as her assent. "Excellent. Miss Watts?"

Jem quavered under his charcoal eyes. "Y-yes."

Merinda punched Ray's arm playfully. "Not so bad, are you, DeLuca? Come on, Jem. Our chaperone has been most valiant and steered us into the safer parts of town." She winked up at Ray. "But we can get home ourselves from here." She grabbed Jem's arm and marched purposefully onward.

Jem turned her head over her shoulder in Ray's direction. He was now leaning against a pole, his unfathomable black eyes focused on his scrap of folded paper. Her heart beat at ten times its normal pace. She couldn't think of one remotely sane or useful thing to say.

I know your secrets, her mind screamed. *I have your journal and I know your beautiful words and that you see the city as I do. I know you miss your first home, but I'm so glad the boat brought you here. To our city, to my city.*

Before she could think better of it, she ran lightly back to where Ray stood watching them. She leaned in and kissed his right cheek.

He felt her butterfly lips on the day-old stubble at his jawline. She stepped back, almost tripping. He stood unwaveringly still, blinking in surprise and confusion.

Jem wanted him to smile, wanted to carry his smile with her, tuck it in her pocket and keep it there to pull out when she needed. So she smiled—broad and wide, in hopes that he would mirror it. She waited, counted a few beats that felt a slight century, and almost despaired of her foolishness.

Then she saw the smile in his eyes. Her heart felt light and she turned on her heel to catch up with Merinda.

Chapter Ten

*There is some inherent intelligence in her face. A
spark constantly lit behind her eyes. She is two
steps ahead of you and has already looked you
over…Perhaps the greatest mystery is why no young
man has snatched either of these girls from their
spinster lives and transplanted them into the realm
of domesticity. Swapping propriety for adventure,
Herringford and Watts are more preoccupied
in their current investigations than in securing
husbands, a fact that may make you working ladies,
bachelor girls, and shoppies stand up and salute.*

The Hogtown Herald

J em whistled as Merinda appeared at the breakfast table the next
morning far earlier than she had ever seen her. Merinda was clad
in a gray cotton dress. She scratched at her collar and announced
her intention to play the part of an out-of-work girl from the Ward at
Spenser's garment workplace.

After breakfast, Merinda followed Jem through her usual morning
commute. But while Jem alighted at Queen and Yonge and crossed
the street to Spenser's, Merinda stayed on a little farther north to
Gerrard.

At the garment workplace, Merinda was led into a dank, overcrowded room that at one point must have been a parlor but had
fallen into grave disarray. Several women were already bent over their

piecework. None smiled or looked up. Few talked, and when they did they kept it a whisper. The forewoman showed her where to hang her coat and place her luncheon bucket. A few women silently inched over to allow her room on a crowded bench. Merinda smiled her thanks, but no one said anything. Instead, she was handed a large pile of soft cloth. Silk.

"You brought your thread and needles?" the forewoman asked. In this regard, Merinda was prepared. She nodded. "And a thimble?" She nodded again. The forewoman continued: "Get a start on these. We keep ten percent of what we sell to cover supplies." She acknowledged the cloth folded in Merinda's lap. "I see that face. Don't worry: You can buy your fill of it. Mr. Spenser provides it to his ladies at cost."

At cost or not, this was a sham, Merinda thought. Women had to pay from their meager salary to provide their own needle and thread, and they were also docked for their fabric—a fabric of a quality far more dear than they could ever afford.

Merinda set to her work. She was a quick learner and watched the perfunctory motions of the women around her. The dingy light through the curtains made it difficult to see the delicate stitches without squinting. She saw several women with crude spectacles and pince-nez.

"Sight is the first thing to go," one of the girls told her. Another girl, who couldn't have been fifteen yet, warned her that bone stiffness and arthritis would eventually set in.

Merinda concentrated on her cloth, wanting to act the part as authentically as possible. She followed the sewing pattern, despite her awareness that there had to be a dozen different ways to cut corners for the same result. Instead, she sewed the desired detail into each shirtwaist. Some ladies around her had beautiful scalloped pieces. She was happy with her plain stitches.

Stealing a glance up now and then, Merinda saw harsh worry lines blighting the girls' faces. Worse still, she saw the callused redness of misshapen fingers. These women worked hard and long hours. They were far more poorly dressed than she was, and she was wearing something third-hand from the trunk. She wondered if they knew anything but twelve-hour shifts and poor pay.

She stitched and threaded and observed. She wove and tangled and spun and spindled. When her lunch break came, she ate on her own, fingering the edge of her shirt and playing with the crust of her sandwich before giving the entire thing to a slack-jawed young Asian woman whose eyes were foggy with hunger.

Then she was back at it. She learned nothing other than the mechanics of a twill stich. At the end of the day, Merinda reached into her pocket and tossed the forewoman enough money to pay for a week's worth of thread for each girl. She had barely survived one shift at this menial and horrible job—how could these women piece and stitch for sixty-five hours a week?

As they stepped into the cold air together, Merinda longed for the warmth she would enjoy by her hearth. But she was painfully aware that these other women would return to barely habitable living situations where they would now be expected to care for their families.

Few spoke English, but she spoke to those who did, asking them about Fiona and Grace, and asserting that she was familiar with the latter from the King Edward laundry. No one wanted to talk about the Morality Squad, though, even in the light way Merinda cast out the line. The Corktown girls? The seamstresses had apparently learned from the tragedy of those murders and were playing it safe. A few admitted to a few trips to the dance hall on Elm. But they cautioned Merinda to keep her hem to regulation length and to ensure she had a male escort.

Merinda was too angry to take the streetcar. She walked instead, wanting to vent her frustration and stretch her cramped muscles.

It took a full city block before she spotted the slight figure close behind her. Merinda turned and made out the pale features of the girl who had eaten her lunch. Poor waif.

Merinda offered a companionable smile. "What can I do for you?" Merinda ruffled in her bag for money.

"I know who you are," the girl said.

"Do you?"

The girl gave a shrill whistle, and another girl of the same height and size materialized, seemingly out of thin air. This one had features not as pronouncedly Asian as her young companion, but there was a similarity in their size and stature.

"I'm Kat. She's Mouse."

Merinda shook each offered hand. "And I am—"

"You're Merinda Herringford," Kat said. "You're that lady detective."

"That's right."

"Word on the street is that you're trying to find who killed those poor Irish girls."

"That would be correct."

Kat and Mouse shared a smile. "You're going to need help," Kat said.

"I have help." Merinda was amused. "I have my associate, Jemima."

"Jemima can't sneak in and around like we can."

"What are you suggesting?"

"Mouse and I know the city like the backs of our hands. You want something done, we do it."

"When you're not sewing shirtwaists?" Merinda raised an eyebrow at Kat, while Mouse remained silent.

"I needed extra coin. But now I have you."

Merinda mulled a moment. It would be helpful to have someone track Montague. Someone to keep an eye on that Forbes fellow from the Morality Squad. To report anything out of the ordinary in the city. "You can be my eyes and ears," she said, understanding.

Kat and Mouse nodded in unison. "Exactly."

Merinda introduced Kat and Mouse to Jem as their Baker Street Irregulars. She provided them with a few wardrobe changes, pleased that their short, flat figures allowed them to easily pass as boys. She set them off to trail Gavin Crawley and Tertius Montague, to watch the headlines, and to let them know what was said about Corktown. They also were invaluable for running errands and messages—especially to Ray in the Ward or at the Hog office—so that Merinda and Jem could focus more on the Corktown case.

Jasper was still miffed to be off the case in which Jem and Merinda were invested. "I know I can't work it any longer," he said one night as he and Merinda sat at dinner and Jem worked late. "But I'm at a loss as to why Station One has let it go completely."

The wheels in Merinda's head turned. "Where are most of the Morality Squad constables from?"

"The ones that aren't plainclothes are from Station One." Jasper turned and smiled at Mrs. Malone as she spooned more soup from the tureen. "Thank you!"

Merinda nodded at this information. "Is it usual for someone of your rank and record to be punished with traffic duty for so long, just for letting two girls close to a crime scene?"

Jasper shook his head slowly. "Lieutenant Riley told me it wasn't from him. It came from Chief Tipton. He's bearing down hard these days. My supervisor fought for me. I know he did."

Merinda chewed this for a moment, then tore off a piece of roll. "Jasper, did it ever occur to you that they may not want the murders solved?"

"Nonsense, Merinda. I have to trust my superiors and respect Chief Tipton's decision. Anyway, it does me good to work the King beat, you know. Keeps my head from getting too big."

Merinda bit her lip to stifle a snicker. "Jasper, you're already the most humble man I know. You know something has to be going on over there. Chief Tipton just closes the door on the Corktown Murders? What if Tipton is in Montague's pocket? He kills these girls and they remove their best detective from the squad. Don't blush, Jasper, it's unbecoming."

"I have more faith in the Toronto Police than that, Merinda. Why would I work for someone who was so obliviously corrupt?"

Merinda didn't want to speculate. All she knew was that it seemed the newspapers were all too eager to move onto far more mundane headlines, like the cooling weather or a looming transit strike, and that the Toronto Police were not in any great hurry to solve the case of two deceased girls. Indeed, the only person who seemed to want to solve the case was her!

That evening, Gavin Crawley was to take Jem to *The House with Closed Shutters,* which was playing over at the Harmonium. He'd planned to pick her up from work, and he arrived at Spenser's with a wink and a smile.

"Gavin," Jem said, "may I present Tippy Carr?"

Tippy's cheeks were bright red. She must have found him as handsome as most women did.

Gavin gave a short laugh. "Odd name."

"It's short for Tabitha," Tippy said, her eyes down at her lap.

Jem looked from one to the other. Did she imagine it, or did a kind of strange energy spark between them? But before she could ponder it, Gavin was taking Jem's arm and escorting her the few blocks to the Harmonium.

The moving picture show was about a woman who posed as a man and fought in the war. *How ironic,* Jem thought. Before she'd met Merinda, such a getup as the actress wore in the movie would have seemed preposterous to Jem. Now, sitting beside Gavin in the dark and recalling her most recent trouser-clad adventure, she was surprised at how much her life had changed. Not only her life but also her worldview. Little surprised her anymore.

"Can you imagine?" Jem gushed after the picture was finished and they went for a soda and ice cream on Wellington Street. "A woman soldier!"

"It's improper!" Gavin said.

"She saves her brother! Sacrifices herself!" Jem's hands flew to her heart. With Gavin by her side and the fizzy soda bubbling at her nose, she could barely contain her euphoria. "Merinda would love that story."

Gavin took a pin to her balloon. "You know I don't approve of your living with Merinda Herringford."

"She's my best friend," Jem offered simply, slurping through her straw.

"You should be married by now."

The soda spurted through her nose, fizzing her nostrils. She coughed. "E-excuse me?"

"You know you should. Pretty girl like you."

He spoke of marriage as if it were easy, or as if he'd said only, "You should have a cat by now." Gavin buried the words under his usual string of compliments, but the aftertaste remained. Before, on lonely nights, she would trace similar words in a romantic novel with her finger, wishing someday, somewhere someone would say them to her. Why, then, did they fall as flat as the fizzed-out soda she was absently twirling with her straw?

Chapter Eleven

*Lately, I have taken to walking by St. James on the way
home. The first time I slipped in I felt immediately that
I was somewhere I shouldn't have been. The beautiful
tiles and polished fixtures. The saints in their rainbow-
glassed vignettes. I just come and clutch my hat in my
hands and sit. One afternoon the minister, Ethan Talbot,
came and spoke to me. He told me that the door will
never be locked for me. Then he offered to teach me
to read and write English. And I promised, in that
moment, I would do something with that gift. Someday.*

From a journal which Jem still (guiltily) has in her possession

R ay sat at his desk in the *Hog* office, transcribing notes he'd
scrawled in his peculiar shorthand the night before. *Cold.
Wretched. A mess of nomads and working men. I have
befriended a Swede, Lars, and am helping him with his English. Wonder
if he'll acquire my Italian accent. Or my penchant for bad poetry.*

As Ray sat typing at his old Underwood, Skip stood nearby rambling a mile a minute about emulsions and exposures, reflectors and
plates, all while cleaning his equipment.

"You hungry, Skip?"

"Possibly."

Ray took him to the Wellington Room just across City Hall.

Skip wasn't nearly as interested in his roast beef sandwich as Ray
was in his. Instead, Skip's eyes focused on the foot traffic out the

window. He boxed his index fingers and thumbs like a lens and peered through. "The entire city is a photograph, Mr. DeLuca."

Ray smiled and chewed slowly.

Skip moved his imaginary lens over the street, finally stopping on a pair of women dressed in white shirtwaists and prim black skirts. "There she is."

Ray swallowed and looked up. "Jemima Watts?"

For there was Jem, presumably on her lunch break, laughing at something her companion had said.

"No," Skip said. "That vision of a girl beside her."

Ray studied her. Doe-eyed and pretty. Fairy-like, almost. He nudged Skip. "You're sweet on her?"

"Her name is Tippy. That's what they call her. I've got a friend who works in the shipping department." He sighed. "She's nice to look at."

Ray leaned across. "You should tell her that."

"'You are nice to look at.'" Skip's voice was monotone as he repeated it. "I've seen her before at one of those dances on Elm Street."

Ray laughed. "*Sei una ragazza carina.*"

Skip brightened. "There. That sounds much better. What does that mean?"

"You are a pretty girl."

"I wish I could say it like you."

"Hmm." Ray smiled as he watched Jem struggling to keep her straw hat atop her head as the wind whisked across the road. "I don't think women want sly or clever, Skip. I'm sure your Tippy would appreciate your telling her the truth."

"You think so?"

Ray gave a dark laugh. "That's your advice from a bachelor reporter." He shrugged ruefully and took another bite of roast beef sandwich.

"Dance with me, Jem." Jasper jumped up from his half-eaten dinner. He set the phonograph to playing and brought Jem to her feet.

He had waltzed into Jem and Merinda's dining room that evening relaying the details of the upcoming Policeman's Ball even through their meal. It was the one night when all men from every station, even lowly detective constables normally on traffic duty, met on common ground in the ballroom at the King Edward Hotel. Jasper vowed to spit-shine his shoes, polish his bronze buttons bright, and whirl the night away.

Jem laughed and smiled shyly at Merinda, who was hardly paying attention. "I'm not in shape here. Haven't danced in years."

"Nonsense. You have a natural grace. And I need to practice." He extended his hand to her.

"Oh, very well!" Jem rose and took his hand. They made great ceremony of bowing to each other.

Jasper proved a proficient enough dancer, though there was something boxed rather than fluid about his careful movements. Jem watched the strain on his face, betraying the counting in his head.

One two three, one two three, one two three.

Jem fell into the easy step of his lead, and after a few spins her head was light. The music and the rapturous mood and their collective laughter kept her in a constant, dizzy carousel until the phonograph squeaked to an abrupt stop.

"I've got it!" Merinda said, standing. "Jasper! Jasper stop!" Merinda was across the room in a flash and grabbing his forearm. Jasper and Jem stopped midstep. "Is the ball sponsored by Mayor Montague again?"

Jasper wiped his forehead. "Yes. And Chief Tipton. All the police will be there, and a few reporters are invited too."

"Good! Jasper, *I* will be your guest." Merinda shoved Jem out of the way and stood in front of Jasper. "Show me how to do this thing you're doing." She waved her hand about.

"Waltzing?"

"Yes."

Merinda waltzing? Jasper and Jem's eyes met, but both managed not to laugh. Jem looked Merinda over, beginning with the braids plaited down her back and ending with the cuffs of the trousers over her rubber-soled boots. There was nothing graceful about Merinda. She was all angles and lines and precision. But, Jem thought, dancing with Jasper *was* more like mapping out the corners of a rigid triangle than spinning weightlessly on clouds.

Jasper cleared his throat and looked suddenly nervous.

Jem took a chair. "This will be very interesting to watch."

"Merinda, have you ever danced before?" asked Jasper.

Merinda scowled. "What do you think?"

Jasper flushed, his eyes sparkling at the glorious prospect of taking Merinda into his arms. "Merinda," he said, "this is going to be difficult for you."

"Difficult?" She laughed at him, gave an exaggerated bow, and mimicked a few of the movements she had seen Jem and Jasper performing before. "See?"

"Yes, well, it's different when you're dancing alone, Merinda," Jem remarked from the sofa.

"How hard can it be?" Merinda asked. "Now, Jasper, do that thing you did."

"What thing, Merinda?"

"Where you bowed to Jem and placed your hand out and looked like one of those fellows in the Spenser's catalogue."

"Like this?" Jasper bowed, rather tersely and unsure, and held out his hand.

"Yes! You don't cut a very dashing figure, but I suppose I am not primed to be the belle of the ball." She laughed lightly, no doubt thinking of the Jasper who hit the top beam of every doorframe, who gleefully inspected the larvae under his microscope on Saturdays, smoky-faced from a botched experiment in the chemistry lab.

But Jem saw Jasper's back straighten. Her words had cut him unintentionally, and now he made to act an even more convincing part. "I can be a gentleman, Merinda."

Jem's heart sank. He was trying so hard.

Merinda, however, remained concentrated on the problem at hand. She moved toward him expectantly, grabbed both his hands with force, and clutched tightly.

"I don't—I say, Merinda, it doesn't need to be as *drastic* as all this!" Jasper was flustered.

"I want to do this right!" And off she went, pushing Jasper backward.

Jasper allowed a few more awkward steps before correcting her. "Merinda, *I* lead."

"Lead?"

"I lead. I...I go first. I guide you. There is no other way to do it. You saw Jem and me do it. You follow my lead."

Merinda mumbled something about the conventions of patriarchy, but Jasper went on: "The most important thing is the count. *One* is pronounced. It is the down count. Then two and three are lifting..." He raised the inflection in his voice. "Much lighter."

"All right! One!" Merinda smashed Jasper's foot, and he stepped back with a yelp. "Sorry, Jasper. Beginner's luck, eh? Let's go again. Ah, I get it ! *One*-two-three. *One*-two-three. All twirly and light on the two-three and...*Jemima!*"

"Yes!"

"Put that silly song on."

"Strauss, Merinda. He's extremely famous."

"Yes, yes. I am sure."

The music swelled. Merinda's eyes latched on to Jasper's. "Lead if you must."

Easier said than done. There were many things Merinda could do, but it seemed that waltzing was not one of them. Especially when it required her unconditional submission to Jasper's directive. She stepped and tripped, stepped and fell. He caught her and spun her, led her, cajoled her. And for a split second, she melted into his arms and the rhythm....

But it didn't last. She laughed and stomped her heel and declared dancing the *silliest pastime*. "Cracker jacks! Can't we just go to the ball and sit it out with punch and finger sandwiches?"

Jem planted her palm to her forehead. "You're not even trying."

"Don't be absurd, Jem," Jasper said mischievously. "She's *very* trying!"

There was something vulnerable and majestic about "The Blue Danube," however, and it worked its magic. Clumsily, Jasper and Merinda made their way through several bars on their seventeenth try. But then, just as the piece melted to legato, the angels winked from above and Merinda finally succumbed to Jasper. They blended, and under his lead she seemed stronger and more graceful than ever. Jasper was spellbound, Merinda was momentarily tamed, and the waltz gave them a moment of crystalline perfection.

The next morning, Jem received three rose blooms and an accompanying notecard. The card was an invitation to accompany Gavin to the Policeman's Ball. Jem's heart did four somersaults, and she squealed and ran to Merinda's room. She jumped on her bed, waking her up.

Merinda mumbled something unintelligible.

"Merinda, I am going to the ball! We're both going to the ball!"

"I don't care, Cinderella. I'm trying to sleep."

Jem shook Merinda's shoulder and pulled her up off her pillow. "We need to go shopping. Both of us."

"Shopping? Not me. I'll rummage in the trunk."

"You will *not* disgrace Jasper with something out of your uncle's smelly trunk. Come. The dance is a week from Saturday. You're playing a part, after all. You're undercover!"

This roused Merinda. She tossed the comforters back and followed Jem to the kitchen.

Dressed and out the door, they rode the streetcar to Spenser's. Jem always enjoyed coming on her days off. She saw so little of the hustle and bustle of the place, so holed away was she in the mailroom.

The ladies' department smelled of lavender. Jem explained their errand to the salesgirls, and they rushed to parade fabric and shirtwaists, gowns and tresses, bustles and shawls. Jem and Merinda were measured and spun.

Merinda's transformation was more overwhelming than Jem's. When Jem stepped from behind a curtained partition to spin in her new gown, her jaw dropped. Merinda, so often hidden in oversized men's clothes and silly jackets and hats, had a beautiful figure offset by the sheer organdy of the dress. She claimed to have chosen it mostly because it had the least ornamentation or "frilly frous."

"Merinda, you look beautiful."

Merinda lifted the dress up over her ankle. "It's too long."

"We can hem it for you, miss. Sarah, will you bring the shoes you found?"

The shoppies showed her a pair of beautiful white shoes, at which she initially scoffed. Jem took them gently from the girl and showed Merinda the inseam and tread. "For waltzing." She winked. "You don't want to trip over Jasper and make a fool of yourself."

Jem turned to see Merinda's inevitable glower, but Merinda was no longer at her side. Moments later, she found her in the men's department, her shoulder pressed against a mannequin dressed in the latest style and cut.

"What are you doing? We need gowns. This is one night when we are *not* going about in trousers and vests!"

"Look who is with Mr. Spenser!" Merinda pointed and Jem looked up. "I'm watching Tony Valari. DeLuca's brother-in-law. He pointed him out to me one time when I was walking by the *Hog*."

"He's not doing anything now but talking. Shopping. Which is what we are supposed to be doing. Come along."

"But DeLuca said Tony often does work for Mayor Montague. And yet here he is with Spenser. Which makes me wonder who's on what side."

"Or if they're both on the same side," Jem added. "Spenser and Montague could just be friends who use the same weasely man to run errands."

"They have money and unfathomable influence, Jemima. They don't *need* friends."

Jem tugged her back in the direction of the ladies' department, and this time she succeeded.

For herself, Jem found a dress and accessories, and then they strolled without purpose through the displays of daysuits and parasols, boots and hats, pearls and buttons. A feminine wonderland.

Jem's mind spun in a recurring daydream wherein she was on Gavin's arm as his wife. Set for life, living in a house with a white picket fence and matching dishes. Jem would spend her days idly responding to correspondence, making luncheon and dinner plans, engaging her social secretary in flippant conversation, and traveling with Gavin across the world. Greece! Cypress! Algiers! The globe at their fingertips.

A strange pang caught in her chest. Five years ago such a marriage might have tempted her. But now...?

Merinda wandered in the direction of straw hats and bowlers, and Jem took a moment at the cosmetics counter, spritzing rosewater on her wrists and peeking into the crystal-framed mirror on the counter. The fluorescent display light caught the laugh lines rimming her eyes. She looked at herself plainly. The Jem that God saw.

"Gavin's got a cracker jack of a girl," she told her reflection.

Chapter Twelve

*Life in Toronto is more difficult than I imagined. Tony
and I canvass the streets daily for odd jobs, barely
scraping enough to buy day-old loaves of bread. I
resented the King Edward Hotel the first time I
saw it. There it sat on grand display with its royally
draped awnings, rimmed with carriages and shiny
automobiles spiriting guests away to highbrow events.
I wondered, for a moment, what it would be like to
be free of the constant gnaw of hunger and worry.*

From a journal that Jem really, really ought to have returned by now

The Crystal Ballroom at the King Edward Hotel was every
bit as magical as its name suggested. The moonlight shone
through the windows and twinkled in the chandeliers high
above their heads. Servers in coattails and white gloves offered champagne in delicate flutes. Ladies fanned themselves and congregated
like bouquets as they awaited the announcement of the next dance.

Jem and Merinda were dressed in a way befitting ladies of their station. Their sleeves were like wispy tulips scalloping their arms, frosted
with jewels.* Their skirts draped to the floor in an almost Grecian
style.

Jasper appeared, clean-pressed, buttons burnished, spit-shone,
and wide-eyed at Merinda's transformation. "Merinda, I..."

That was as far as his sentence got. Firstly, because Jasper lost his

---

* The jewels, of course, were costume pieces from their old trunk on King Street.

breath completely, and secondly, because the conductor started the easy three-step movement of the waltz.

Gavin Crawley, appearing like a fairytale prince, held his hand out for Jem, giving her a slight bow before straightening his shoulders in a trim line. His lips found her ear and he said something about Jem being a glowing jewel. He lifted her hand and kissed it, and they joined Merinda and Jasper on the dance floor.

The circular repetition of the waltz and Jem's enchantment at the people spilling in out of the sparkling room left little chance for Jem to begin a conversation. When the dance spun to its final, lingering bar, Jem stopped only to catch her breath before the strings pulsed and they were tripped back into their routine.

Finally, they were allowed a respite, and Gavin linked Jem's arm through his. "Would you like some champagne, Jem?"

"That would be lovely, Gavin."

He bade her wait a moment, and he soon returned with a bottle of bubbling liquid and two glasses. "It's a beautiful night," he said. "Let's take this outside."

Jem breathed freely once they stepped out onto King Street. The lights from Yonge winked over the rooftops and billboards and blended with the starlight. "I love the city at night," she said with a shiver. She had her wrap, which wouldn't be enough to stay the winter chill, but her heart was beating and a swoosh of frosty air was a welcome reprieve from the crowded ballroom.

Gavin poured the champagne and set the bottle on the ground beside him. They were at the edge of the street. Nearby, the bells of St. James cathedral tolled ten. "Do you think there is such a thing as a witching hour, Jemima?" Gavin asked as they clinked their glasses with a crystal *ting*.

"A witching hour?"

"When everything becomes magical," Gavin said, tracing Jem's cheek with his fingers. "And anything"—he leaned closer—"becomes possible."

Jem steadied herself. Gavin's fingers explored the back of her hair and trailed down her neck and to the backless scoop of her dress beneath her wrap. "That tickles." Jem took another sip.

"Let's try another sensation, shall we?" Gavin moved his mouth closer so it hovered just above hers, his breath whispering over her chin. He leaned forward.

Jem stopped him with a hand on his chest. "No, thank you, Gavin."

He didn't pull away. "We're not doing anything wrong."

"I'm a traditional girl."

"You wear trousers all over Toronto and skulk around murder scenes." He went for another kiss, and she turned away.

"Neither of those things involves kissing!" Jem protested.

Gavin's voice soured. "How old-fashioned are you, exactly?"

Jem adjusted her stole. "It's pathetically romantic, I'm sure. But I intend that the first man I kiss will be the man I marry."

"Oh," he said, and took a long drink from his glass. "But perhaps if you tried it…" Gavin leaned in again and Jem smelled again the tang of champagne and his heady cologne.

She turned her head to the side. "I've had a wonderful time dancing with you, Gavin."

"Dancing?" Gavin reached into his breast pocket and extracted a cigar. "Do you mind?"

Jem shook her head.

He unwrapped the cigar and pressed it to his lips. From another pocket he took a match, scraped it on the concrete to light it, and lit his cigar.

"I know that smell," Jem said. "Must be my father's brand."

"Wellington? Your father has good taste."

Jem still hadn't tired of the cool breeze. And with Gavin smoking—not kissing—she fell into the euphoria of the night air, the champagne, the dancing, and her handsome escort.

A very handsome escort who, at that very moment, was leaning in again and maneuvering for a kiss. She hadn't noticed him putting out his cigar. And now he grabbed her around the waist. "Oh, Jem." Truant fingers explored her collarbone.

"Stop it, Gavin," Jem exploded. "How many times do I have to tell you?"

He kept her pulled close to him. "We're not doing anything wrong. We're perfectly respectable. How long will you be waiting?"

Jem gritted her teeth. "It might seem a stupid hill to die on." She pushed him back. "But die on it I will."

"Please."

"Listen, Mr. Morality Squad, I am surprised at how hypocritical you're acting!"

"And I am surprised at what a tease you're being!"

"Me? A tease? You're a cad!"

He growled at the sky. "I'm freezing." Gavin grabbed the bottle of champagne and bounded off toward the hotel, leaving Jem alone on the street.

She headed toward St. James cathedral, which was not far away. Late-night revelers gave her a chorus of wolf whistles and howls as they headed to the nearest pub. Jem knew that as soon as she reached the church, all of the tension pent up in her chest would be released. Her body, which had felt so light while dancing, was suddenly weighed down with the memory of Gavin's touch. Her nostrils couldn't shake the smell of smoke and alcohol.

Jem reached the church just as she was reminding herself she wasn't getting any younger. She dropped onto the park bench out front, drew her knees to her chest in a most unladylike fashion, and fixed her eyes on the steeple piercing the starlight overhead. For all her modern views, she held onto a few outlandishly traditional ones. And was it doing her any favors? Maybe a girl who wanted to secure a marriage had to kiss a man whenever he wanted to.

Not that she wanted to marry Gavin, she realized with a start. Not after tonight. Gavin was handsome and well off, but his forward behavior at the ball had changed something in her. Or shown her what she already knew: Gavin Crawley failed to stir her in the same way someone else did.

Someone who, at this very moment, was suddenly behind her.

"I'd kiss you," Ray said, "but I think that would mean I'd have to marry you."

Jem startled upright. "Ray!"

Ray came around her bench and gave a little, flourished bow. He placed his bowler back on his head and sat down beside her.

"How are you everywhere? How?"

Ray spread his hands. "The Policeman's Ball is of endless interest to me. Tertius Montague and Chief Tipton in the same room." He stopped and laughed. "Or maybe I just wanted to see Merinda Herringford in a ball gown."

"You heard everything." Jem melted to a puddle.

"I was behind you, just outside the hotel, taking the air. I saw you with Gavin and I didn't want to disturb you two. But then I thought I was going to have to disturb you. Then I heard him speak and I remembered…" His half-smile appeared.

"You remembered what?"

"That you're not a girl who is going to fall for a line with *witching hour* in it."

Jem smiled ruefully. "It's not such a bad line."

"It's a terrible line." He inclined his chin. "Then, when you plunged off into the night all alone, I figured someone should look out for you."

It felt wonderful, somehow, to know he'd been there, watching over her. But she wouldn't let him know that. Instead, she said, "Very well, Ray, what line would you use?"*

"If I tell you, you're going to want to kiss me."

She raised an eyebrow. "It's that good, is it?"

"It's that good. You'll try to kiss me and I won't be able to stop you. Then I'll have to marry you." He winked. "I know how this works."

Jem pretended to scowl. "So you will only sit there flirting with me."

Ray crossed his arms over his chest. "I'm not flirting."

---

* The astute reader will observe that Jem had long since stopped standing on ceremony and addressed Ray by his given name.

"I don't believe you."

He didn't dignify her with a response. "Do you know what the problem with the English language is, Jemima? It's too fast. It speeds along like the trolleys. My language sounds faster because it has more vowels, but it takes longer to work your mouth around words." He was, indeed, looking at her mouth. She was looking at his. They simultaneously moved their eyes away. "So it should be with wooing a girl," Ray said, a little more slowly.

"Did you just say *wooing*?"

"It can't be fast. You want to taste it. It has to be slow. Methodical. Like poetry."

Jem's mind went to the terrible poetry in his journal. It put a smile on her face that Ray failed to decipher. "Like poetry?" she repeated.

"First," he said, his hands moving languidly, "I would compliment the woman." He took his hat off and bent his head slightly. "The wooing experience should be for her, first and foremost."

The moon shadows spilling through the tree above their bench made his hair seem almost purple. Jem wasn't sure if she could trust her voice to speak again. So she let him continue.

"I would use a term of endearment," he explained. "I would call you *cara mia* or perhaps *bella,* noting that you are beautiful." He said it clinically, dispassionately, Jem noticed, and wondered how he could keep his voice so even when her heart was beating so loudly she was sure he would make out its loud thrum.

Ray nudged his hat toward her. "Nothing too general, though. The sentence should begin and end with your name. To speak of a witching hour is a fool's gambit. It is plain. It could apply to anyone, anywhere. If it were *me* wooing you, Jem, I would want *you* to know that I was lost only in you, and thinking only of you. I would remark on what you were wearing or your hair or your eyes or your voice, or better, something shared just between the two of us."

Jem couldn't tell if he had moved closer or if she was just more aware of him. She had taken off her wrap and settled it in her lap, and it gave her fingers a nice object to grasp, since they shook softly every time he spoke.

"I bet every man who has tried to make love to you has said something about your name and matched it with a jewel," he said. "Or a pretty gem."

Jem couldn't disagree.

"Ah, but it's too easy," he said. "Too predictable. I bet they would say something about your hair. So rich…like a *castagno*…the trees."

"I've heard that before, yes." From a suitor her parents had picked out, Jem remembered. But she wasn't about to tell him that, before Gavin Crawley's crude behavior at the hotel, she hadn't heard anything of the sort for a very, very long time.

"Your eyes. *La stele sono gelose di voi.*"

Jem gave a short breath as her feet dropped to the ground, taking her heart with them. "Say that again."

He obliged, then he translated: "The stars are jealous of you."

"That's a good line." She breathed.

"No!" He wagged his finger at her nose. "Don't fall for such a common line, Jemima. Those are the words of a man who will kiss you and not marry you."

His words were so lovely, his face so handsome, his eyes so black, and his hands so close. "Because he compared my eyes to starlight?"

"Exactly. A man should not use on you what he would use on any other girl. He needs to say something so that you know that he knows you are special. And the gems and the stars—*anyone* can talk about them."

Champagne had nothing on the closeness of this man and his beautiful voice. Why, it made her thoughts spin and her heart gallop. She was just beginning to coax a sentence from her mouth when he spoke again.

"*Io ti preferisco in pantaloni,*" he said. She didn't know what it meant, but it was opera to her. "That is my line for you," Ray whispered. "Just for us. But I should frame it better, no?" He stood before

her and gave a little bow, then got down on one knee and swept his
bowler hat over his chest. "*Io ti preferisco in pantaloni!*"

Jem wasn't sure she had even a sliver of heart left. Had she given
it all to him? And here he was repeating his line. For all she knew, he
could be talking about chocolate or squirrels or knitwear, and yet it
was the most perfect thing she had ever heard.

His eyes stayed with her a long, long time. Then wordlessly he rose,
put his hat back on his head, and strode away.

"You never translated!" she called after him.

"You'll just have to learn Italian," he said without looking back.

Still under the spell of the King Edward, Jasper and Merinda
had maneuvered close to Chief Tipton and Tertius Montague. They
straightened their backs against the wall, pretending to observe the
couples.

"Ah, Officer Forth," Tipton said, approaching with a glass of
champagne.

Jasper stood at attention. "Sir."

Tipton pointed an accusing finger at his breast. "Lucky you're a
corker of a cop."

"Yes, sir."

"Come, Mr. Mayor. Meet young Forth, one of our finest
investigators."

Mayor Montague approached and shook Jasper's hand. "Ah, yes.
I recognize your face, young man." Tipton noticed Merinda. "Now,
Forth, do introduce us to your young lady."

Jasper coughed. The name *Merinda Herringford* had so often been
trumpeted across the front page of the *Hog* that it would not be well
received here.

"Harrison. Annie Harrison," said Merinda. She held out her hand
and used a name from a Doyle story.

Montague raised it to his lips. "Charmed, Miss Harrison."

As soon as propriety allowed, Jasper and Merinda disengaged themselves and returned to the dance floor. Jasper smiled, watching her. "You're really quite a wonderful dancer."

Merinda brightened at the compliment. "Do you think so?"

Jasper nodded. As the dance ended, they spotted Jem and motioned her over.

"Where is Gavin?" Jasper asked.

"My escort is a cad," Jem said.

"But you're smiling." Jasper was perplexed.

Jem blushed. "Am I?"

Merinda leaned across Jasper. "You're very much smiling, Jem."

Jem tried to straighten her mouth. To no avail.

"What say we head home?" Merinda asked.

Jasper and Jem nodded in unison.

A moment later, they were down the stairs and at the street. They were hailing a cab when Jem stumbled into a face she knew well.

"Tippy? What are you doing here? It's midnight!"

Tippy's eyes were red and her arms hugged her chest. "Did you have a nice evening with your escort, Jemima?"

"Not really. He's not with me, as you can see. I am going home with my friends."

Jasper and Merinda gathered themselves into the taxi, but Jem held back with Tippy.

"What's bothering you, Tippy?"

"You could have any man you want, Jemima Watts." Tippy's bottom lip trembled. "That fellow from the *Hog*. Anyone, really."

"Tippy, have you been drinking? Jasper! Hold up a minute. Come, Tippy. Let me take you home. Come on, we'll take you."

Tippy shook her head.

Jem placed a hand on her shoulder. "Tippy, please. You can come back to our flat if you need to."

"Let go of me!" Tippy squirmed away and ran down the street.

Jem watched her go, then ducked into the cab.

"What was that?" Jasper wondered as the cab rambled along. Jem peeked out the window, but Tippy's figure grew smaller until she was nothing but a shadowy speck against the streetlights.

CHAPTER THIRTEEN

An investigator will quickly learn that the most stalwart allies can be found in the most unlikely places

Guide to the Criminal and Commonplace, M.C. Wheaton

The days started to yawn longer as the city readied itself for a spring that would come eventually, despite the pervading chill and continual snow. Ray was peering out at the dim sun and could hear Skip packing up his camera equipment for the night.

Ray heard the door creak open and peeked around the slat bordering his cubby to see Jasper Forth, hat tucked under his arm, cordial smile wide.

"I'm looking for Mr. DeLuca." His voice was as jovial as his face.

Skip pointed toward Ray's office area, and Jasper ducked to miss a low extending beam.

"And here I thought you were on probation." Ray stood and extended a hand blackened with ink. He noticed Jasper taking in his surroundings. "Quite a place, yes? This is what happens when you turn an abandoned distillery into a newspaper, Detective Constable Forth."

"Just 'Constable' now."

Ray ignored him. "Detective Constable, you're the only investigator who would have pursued the Corktown case. And now it's wide open. Have a seat." Ray used the toe of his scuffed shoe to kick a crate across the floor, and Jasper sat on it. "You really think you were kicked back to the traffic beat because you brought Merinda Herringford to a crime scene?"

"I couldn't be sure. It was the explanation they gave."

"No. Chief Tipton saw Montague's name in connection with the crime and became petrified. You might have named him a suspect, so you had to be removed."

"You think Montague is the killer?"

Ray shrugged. "All I can see is that a lot of people are"—he pulled a phrase from the air—"covering their tracks."

Jasper ran his hand through his hair. "And St. Joseph's Home for Working Men? You've been writing about it quite a bit lately. What's the connection?"

Ray was impressed and smiled. "You read my paper!" He spread his palms on his knees. "It's a Montague-run establishment. Investigating it is keeping me employed. McCormick wants more pieces like that Don Jail exposé. Apparently, trailing Merinda Herringford around Toronto is not news enough."

Jasper studied Ray's face. "That's not all you know about St. Joseph's, is it?"

Ray cocked his head. "Can I trust you?"

"I hope so."

Ray looked around the office, as if spies might be lurking in the shadows. "St. Joseph's is full of vulnerable prey: men who are easily coaxed into doing the Morality Squad's buffoonish work and laundering money at the tracks. They take their chances and do the work in order to keep Montague's hands clean."

"All of them?"

"No. Not all. It's a legitimate establishment in ways. Some men living there are just trying to get by." Ray smiled. "Did you come here to talk about Montague, truly?"

"No." Jasper seemed to be choosing his words carefully. "I came to talk about your exclusive Herringford and Watts connection."

Ray leaned on the back legs of his chair and rocked. "You're Merinda's keeper?"

He shook his head. "A concerned friend."

"Concerned?"

"You encourage them. With your articles. She is over the moon to be officially represented in the *Hog*. You validate the whole experience."

Ray shrugged. "They interest me."

"They are girls in bowler hats and men's trousers." Jasper seemed exasperated.

"I thought you were helping them. Merinda told me that you'd been allowing them to trail your cases."

"She nearly trips over my shoes following me."

Ray leaned forward until his chair rested on all four legs again. "I suppose I was wrong about your relationship."

"I'm not...she's not..." Jasper coughed and rearranged the brim of his hat. "Our association is strictly professional. I respect Merinda."

"As you should."

"I know things about Montague's Morality Squad."

Ray kept his expression unchanged. "As do I. I room with half of them. But I don't know what you're getting at."

"Merinda needs watching, and she drags Jem along with her. In this case, you and I both know they are in over their heads. Merinda would take a bullet for Jem, but I don't want her to have to." Jasper exhaled.

"Agreed. But I don't think, as you do, that they play at detective as at some children's game."

"You seem to say as much in your articles," Jasper said.

"I try to keep my tone light. I want to feature them so that people know they are available to help without posing them as an actual threat to Mayor Montague's anti-female brigade."

"Jem has the right idea. She's pursuing a sane, useful, safe profession at Spenser's."

"Yes," Ray said, "right up until the moment she darts off and follows her friend. Tell me, Detective Constable Forth, would you pursue Merinda's friendship so ardently if she only knit socks and aided the church bazaar?"

Jasper mulled over the question a moment, his eyes drifting over scrap paper sporting tomorrow's headlines. "She was going to be a doctor. She's a great scientist."

"And Ms. Watts?"

"Conditioned to be a wife. Raised in appropriate circles. She's beautiful, gentle, and committed to appropriate accomplishments. At least she was until Merinda got her claws into her."

"I should write all this down," said Ray, crossing his hands behind his head. "Publish it in the *Hog*. The origin of our bachelor girl detectives."

"But you won't," Jasper said.

Ray smiled. "No, I won't, because I'd very much like you on my side. I don't have many friends, and definitely not very many among the police. You must think my work on this rag is the lowest of the sort. Scraping the mire."

"You couldn't be more wrong. You have the audacity to seek out what no one else will. And you're pursuing the Corktown case, as I wish I could." Jasper sighed. "I can't expect you to stop Merinda. Truthfully, if you stopped running articles about their adventures, she would find somewhere else to get word out about them."

"So what are you asking?"

"I suppose I'm asking you to watch out for them."

"Detective Constable Forth, I already am."

After Jasper had exited, Ray went back to his desk. He'd barely settled in when Skip appeared, his face grave. "You look like you've seen a ghost!"

"This was in the post." Skip silently held a slip of paper out to Ray. "No envelope or anything."

Ray spread it out on his desk. Clippings of words in several different fonts, obviously pulled from different newspapers, had been pasted together. Some bold and in full caps as if from a headline, others small.

Stop covering the Corktown Murders! was spelled in the largest letters. Other text followed in smaller print.

Ray whistled. "Well, nice threat!"

"Take it seriously, Mr. DeLuca." Skip snapped in front of Ray's face. "Do what it says: Stop covering the Corktown Murders! I don't want this fellow to come after you. Or me. Especially not me."

"Ah, yes." Ray read over the rest of the letter and lingered on the last sentence. "I am also ordered to stop reporting the detecting adventures of the Misses Herringford and Watts." Ray bit his lip and took a look around the office.

Skip watched him warily. "What are you thinking?"

By way of answer, Ray grabbed his coat and set out into the snow.

"Where are you going?" Skip called after him.

"To buy every paper I can get my hands on until I find out where this is from and who sent it."

Five cold minutes later, Ray stumbled upon a newsboy who was crying the evening headlines on the corner of Queen Street. When he approached, he realized the newsboy was, in fact, a newsgirl. Ray recognized her as one of the pair that did Merinda Herringford's bidding. "You almost finished here?" he asked her.

She widened her dark eyes in an attempt to look more innocent even than her smudged cheeks and quivering lip were doing. "Buy a paper?" She put on a good show. No doubt she made a good living at it.

Ray reached into his coat pocket. "Go get your friend and buy all the papers." He retrieved a few coins and placed them in her hand.

"My friend?"

"Your partner. The other girl. Look, I'm a friend of Miss Herringford's. I know who you are and what you do for her. Buy them all, a copy of every paper, and take them to Miss Herringford's."

Not much later, Ray and Merinda were sitting at the dining room table at King Street, hunched over the bounty of Kat and Mouse's endeavor. Merinda walked to the bureau and retrieved one of the threatening letters Tippy had received. Sure enough, they were the same style.

"Do you see how the slight, uneven frays at the side of each cut letter are left, not right?" Merinda asked Ray. "It stands to reason that a left-handed person would hold a knife or scissors in his left hand. Especially for a purpose like this one."

"Left handed?"

Merinda's eyes went to the blackboard.

Ray's gaze followed. He noticed his name first on the list of Corktown Murder suspects. He cocked his head with a smile at her. "I was your primary suspect for the murders?"

"What?" Merinda was defensive. "We struck you out."

"I thank you."

"So which of our suspects is left handed? Could it be one of them?"

"Who knows about all of them?" Ray said. "I do know that Tony is right handed."

"And Forbes was toasting people with his right hand at the bar that night. We usually toast with our dominant hand."

Ray studied the other names on the board. "I couldn't tell you about Montague, though."

"And it doesn't rule out Tony or Forbes being responsible for the murders. It just means that neither of them are responsible for this letter," said Merinda.

"Gavin Crawley?"

"Left. That is, he holds his teacup in his left hand." Merinda squinted, then shook her head. "Busy tonight, DeLuca?"

Ray laughed. "You're about to propose something, aren't you."

"We're breaking into the *Globe*. I want to scout out Gavin's office."

Ray raised an eyebrow. "You know what hours we reporters keep. How do you know the intrepid Mr. Crawley won't be in his office?"

"Because Jem will be entertaining him."

Ray's eyebrow rose even higher.

"Oh, posh. You know I didn't mean anything salacious. I meant dinner. She's going to ask him to have dinner with her."

"I'll meet you at eight."

Ray gave her a half smile and Mrs. Malone showed him out.

Merinda impatiently waited by the fire until Jem got home, and then she pounced on her. "Jem, Jem, Jem, I need a favor!"

"For goodness sake, Merinda, I don't even have my coat off yet!"

"You need to go out with Gavin Crawley tonight."

"Ha! Don't you remember, Merinda? We had a row. He assaulted me! Gavin Crawley is a cad, and I shall never spend a moment in his company again."

Merinda lifted a finger. "That's the point, isn't it, Jem? He's a true cad. And most likely linked to the Corktown Murders."

"You have no proof of that."

"That's why you must go out with him. You must distract him so DeLuca and I can break into his office."

"I will not," Jem said, swallowing the envy that arose at the thought of Merinda on an adventure with Ray. "Why don't you go out with Gavin, and I'll go to the *Globe* with Ray?"

Merinda shot her a look. "It's dishonest." Jem added lamely.

"No. It's an investigation."

Jem folded her arms and pursed her lips.

"Jemima," Merinda said softly, "I thought you cared about Tippy. And Brigid."

"Of course I care. But there has to be another way."

"How can you say you care if you're leaving a killer out there on the streets? Free to kill again. What if he comes here, Jem? What if he threatens you, or me, or Mrs. Malone?"

Jem shut her eyes, and Merinda knew she had won.

"So...what?" Jem said. "I'm supposed to telephone that vile cad and ask *him* to take me out? What message will that send, I ask you?"

"I don't care if you send him chocolates laced with arsenic, so long as you keep him out of his office long enough for me to get what I need."

And thus it was that, though determined to toss Gavin Crawley away like a shirt to be laundered, Jem was coerced to coax him to dinner. Merinda could hear half of their telephone conversation from the sitting room. Jem said she would like to give him a second chance. She was a terrible liar, Merinda thought, but Gavin wouldn't hear anything his ego didn't want him to hear.

When the appointed hour arrived, Gavin presented Jem with an ostentatious bouquet of lilies and helped her into his car. Merinda pretended not to see the look Jem shot her as they left.

Ray arrived not long after. "In trousers this evening, I see," he said to Merinda.

"And you're all in black."

"I couldn't very well wear my street clothes to a break-in," he said with a smirk. "I've got to look the part." But then he turned serious. "I still don't like that you're using Jem as a trap."

"Jealousy doesn't become you, DeLuca. Come on."

As they stopped under a streetlamp, she revealed to him that her walking stick was, in fact, a crowbar. She rapped it over the palm of her right hand.

Ray chuckled. "Merinda." As if the name itself defined her endless surprises.

"And these." She jangled keys. "Picklocks I got in Kensington Market."

Ray inspected them, sure she couldn't have acquired them by legal means. "So, with these gadgets and our wits we will break into the *Globe* office in pursuit of...what, exactly?"

"We'll know it when we see it. Come on. We have hours. Jemima's using her feminine wiles or something."

Ray nodded. His skin was still crawling as he thought of the way that brute had pulled Jem so tightly to himself at the Policeman's Ball.

Merinda waved a hand before his eyes. "Are you with me, DeLuca?"

He looked her up and down, took in everything from her bowler hat to her men's shoes. "You know you could get arrested at any moment." He said. "And where would that leave me?"

"Oh, hush. In moments like these I don't know why we let men into the operation in the first place!"

"*You* asked me!" Ray said emphatically, then gave a resigned sigh. "There's a Victoria Street entrance we can use. Off Agnes. The door that leads to the presses should be open. Then it's just a matter of sneaking around to the offices."

A short trolley ride later, they were standing before the *Globe* offices.

It was easy to get in, as Ray had predicted. He delighted at the smells tickling his nostrils. A *real* newspaper! Not the silly old *Hog* drenched with the tang of old hops, barley, and bitters. He had half a mind to break from Merinda and explore.

Merinda reached into her breast pocket and extracted an electric torch she had purchased with her Christmas allowance money.* They used the light to guide their steps toward Gavin Crawley's office. Ray kept watch as Merinda used her new lockset. She got it on the fourth try and, though it was hard to see through the veil of dark, he could sense her Cheshire grin stretching wide.

They explored the office, shuffling through the desk and behind the photographs and framed pictures adorning the room, careful to leave everything in order. Surely there was something here that would prove their suspicion that there was more to the *Globe's* absence of the murder reports than met the eye. They neared a broad, black cabinet. It was here that the crowbar-walking stick came into play. They creaked the shelves open, revealing several files.

Ray and Merinda splayed them on Gavin's neat desk. They thumbed through the files until Merinda's fingers were as black as Ray's.

"Cracker jacks! Here we go!"

"What?"

"Corktown. A whole file on Corktown."

---

* Mr. and Mrs. Herringford were far more accepting of Merinda's eccentricities than Jem's parents were of their well-bred daughter's. As such, Merinda enjoyed financial support as well as generous checks at major holidays.

Reports, unpublished photographs, scribbles, scrawls, and type-face. Red-blotted edits and stories never printed. Theories and quotes. Police reports.

Ray and Merinda skimmed the bylines of the writers of the various articles. Several of these reporters were well known. And none of the articles had been penned by Gavin Crawley.

"The biggest story in Toronto," Ray mused, "and its star journalist lets everything rot in a filing cabinet. Not only do the stories not get published, he himself didn't write about it at all."

Merinda's eyes glowed eerily in the ribbon of torchlight. "It looks like Waverley did his job as editor. There was a big story, and he covered it. He assigned his writers to document every aspect of the murders and the investigation. But they never ran." She showed him a sheet that appeared to be a sort of roster, laying out who would go where and when and how to report on the murders and the police actions.

Ray's eyes narrowed. "It's so organized. This is good reporting."

"Too bad it never saw the light of day."

They halted at the sound of shuffling feet in the corridor beyond. Merinda clicked off the light and stacked the papers and photographs messily into the folder. Ray grabbed Merinda's shoulder and pushed her down beside him behind the desk. Merinda impulsively snatched the folder, popping up like a jack-in-the-box before Ray pulled her down again.

They crouched, listening, as the door clicked open and a slight breeze whispered through the air. From their position beneath the desk, they could see a man's feet stepping carefully. They heard the cabinet shuffle and jangle. Next the papers were rustled about.

"Would be nice if I could see anything," the man's voice said.

Ray knew that voice. He touched Merinda's shoulder and mouthed, *Tony.*

Another man spoke. "This is what you call keeping an eye on the place, Valari?"

Merinda and Ray started simultaneously. Merinda kept her hand clutched on Ray's sleeve.

"I swear," Tony said, "there was no one here before me. I've been standing in the blasted cold for three hours."

"On Yonge?"

"Yes, on Yonge."

"So you've had no one casing Victoria!" The voice seethed anger.

"I can't be everywhere," said Tony.

The second man growled. "Didn't you find it yet?"

"I can't find it."

"A whole file? In Crawley's office? It can't be that hard to find." The unrecognizable voice growled. "Well, we have to clean this up."

"He made us come here on account of his having a prior commitment and not wanting to wait one more night. He can clean it up himself."

"What's so urgent anyways?"

"Maybe he's starting to realize that some of this might creep up on him sooner than later."

Ray and Merinda heard the cabinet close and saw the yellow light of a lantern stream the perimeter of the desk. Finally, Tony and his companion agreed that "someone" was not going to be happy, and they clicked the door shut behind them.

Ray and Merinda exhaled. Ray slowly rose to ensure they were again alone.

The filing cabinet was in shambles and the desktop had been cleared of papers. "Looks like you snitched what they needed just in time," Ray said quietly.

"At least we had the decency to be neat about it," Merinda scoffed, noting the shambles and state of disarray.

Ray leafed through the remaining files, typed pieces, and headlines. "As neat as we could be."

"Let's go," Merinda said, tucking the folder under her arm.

Outside and safely out of sight, they took relieved gulps of air.

"Well," said Merinda.

"Well," said Ray.

"Well, now we know for sure that Tony is involved," Merinda said.

"I like Gavin Crawley even less now," Ray said. "Obviously they are working for him. They are hiding everything they'd uncovered about the murders, and I am not sure why." He shook his head. "Do you think the other man was Forbes?"

"Could be."

Ray whistled lowly. "If Tony and Forbes are affiliated with Gavin, then something isn't right."

"Jem will be finished with her outing soon," Merinda said. "We'll tell her all about this as soon as she gets back."

"At the Bachelor Girl detective office," Ray mused as Mrs. Malone took his coat.

Merinda tugged her blonde curls from under her bowler and shook her head in front of the sitting room fire, asking Mrs. Malone for Turkish coffee and sandwiches. "You drink coffee, DeLuca?"

Ray nodded.

The door creaked open, and Jemima came in. She worked the gloves off her hands and draped her coat over the settee.

"Ray!" she said, not seeing Merinda at all. "How was your sleuthing? Did you find our murderer?"

"We're on the trail, I think," said Merinda. She handed Jem the folder, and she and Ray tripped over each other to relate all the details as Jem leafed through the papers inside. "Thanks for keeping Crawley occupied. His thugs were there, but we beat them to it."

Mrs. Malone interrupted and smiled down at Ray as she poured him coffee. The side of his mouth turned up an inch toward his cheek.

"Thank you," he said.

"These sandwiches are watercress and tuna, and these are lemon curd," she said, indicating the tray she'd placed in front of them. "Which would you prefer?"

"Lemon." He picked one up and popped it in his mouth.

Jem watched him taste it, and something magical happened. His face broke into a broad, uninhibited grin, a smile that could stop clocks and tell the robins it was time to sing. Jem's breath caught in her chest. Certain that Merinda wasn't paying attention, she dared to prolong her look. That smile lit his entire face. If lemon curd got a smile like that, she'd commence keeping a bucketload of it in the pantry!

But all too soon the smile vanished as Ray studied the papers on the table. "Your beau," he said to Jem pointedly after a swallow, "had all the *Globe* articles on the Corktown case."

"He's not my beau." Jem followed Ray's eyes to the papers on the table. "What does it all say?"

"That they assume whoever did the deed is long gone."

"Gone from where? And how?"

"Listen here." Ray grabbed another sandwich and picked up a sheet of paper from the file. "'The one thing Toronto can count on is the efforts of its police service and its nearly spotless track record. Chief of Police Henry Tipton, when approached by our reporter, affirmed that he retained his utmost faith in the department, despite this most grievous open case.'" Ray stopped and popped a little sandwich in his mouth.

"But then they just washed their hands of it?" Jem looked at Merinda, who was rifling through the folder. "Isn't there some sort of journalistic integrity that dictates things *have* to have coverage? Especially something as big as a murder?"

"Two murders!" Ray said. "But Jem, editors have control and if they don't want to publish something, they don't have to. They can choose to cover other stories. In this case, the editor did want to cover this story, and the articles were written. But someone above the editor made sure they never ran. And they all ended up in a folder in Gavin Crawley's office."

Jem was puzzled. "So Toronto's biggest newspaper just decided to leave Corktown out of it? For what reason?"

"For this reason!" Merinda said suddenly. At the very bottom of the file, stuck between two sheets of paper, a graph had caught her eye. She fished it out and laid it on the table. "It would seem," she said, her eyebrows rising, "Gavin Crawley owes certain people a large sum of money."

*In order to ensure that the subject of one's heart's desire
is aware of one's affection, a bachelor girl is encouraged
to undertake a broad gesture. Men are often not as
observant in this area as women would like them to be.*

Dorothea Fairfax's Handbook to Bachelor Girlhood

La Mariage de Figaro—Mozart's joyfully comedic exposition of marriage, love, lust, and masked confusion told in a colorful and zestily silly plot. Jem sat in her excellent side box taking in the buzz of conversation from the audience below. Gavin was dressed to the nines: coattails, a top hat he'd handed to the usher, a pristine white shirt, and gold cufflinks that winked in the bright electric lights.

She couldn't *believe* she had to spend another evening with him. When would Merinda let her end things with this cad once and for all?

"You know Jemima," he was saying as the lights dimmed, "your eyes indeed rival the stars tonight. Bright. Just like gems."

Jem nodded distractedly, even while feigning the smiles and nods that invited further compliment. "Thank you."

He continued murmuring in her ear even as the opera began. By intermission, Jem was bored in spite of the Mozart and the glamour. She hadn't realized that one could get so tired of flattery. She sipped champagne and smiled politely at him until a dark figure entered the box and passed him a message.

Gavin read the note and rose. He said he would be late for the second act but that Jem should go ahead and enjoy it until, upon his return, he would whisk her away for a cup of tea at the café.

Without Gavin weighing her down, Jem floated on air with Mozart. Gavin returned just as the prima donna received an immense bouquet and the curtain fell.

"That was a magical night," she said as Gavin led her from the box. She could feel his hand on the small of her back. And instead of heading for the exit, Gavin steered her toward the wings beyond the gold sconces, ornamentation, gilded wall plasterings, and marble proscenium arch.

"A tour," he said with a smile. "I thought you might want to see where it all comes to life. I'm a patron, you know. Perhaps we can meet the prima donna herself!"

"How wonderful!" Jem was elated and a little nervous as they ducked behind the russet curtain. It smelled of grease and smoke from the recently extinguished lanterns. A tangle of ropes hung from the rafters, and levers and pulleys adorned the black walls.

Several backstage workers tipped their hats to Jem, but they kept their eyes down from meeting Gavin's gaze. Jem surmised he had been back there before. Perhaps with some other woman?

He pulled her hand gently toward stage left and slipped the curtain open just enough so they could watch the last audience members leaving their seats and the orchestra packing up their instruments in the pit below. Gavin's arm tightened around Jem's waist.

"Would you like one of the stagehands to explain all of these mechanizations?"

A crack, a pop, a thud, and a figure emerged from a beam overhead and down a swinging ladder. Jem stared, recognizing Ray—who she had supposed was doing something investigative with Merinda while she entertained Gavin. But instead he was grinning and wiping his hands on his pants.

Jem felt her eyes widen. "Ray, what are you doing here? What were you doing up *there?*"

Ray tipped his bowler. "Miss Watts."

Gavin drew himself up. "Ray DeLuca of the *Hogwash Herald.* What's the meaning of this? I could have you arrested for trespassing."

Ray produced a notebook from his jacket pocket. "Press night," Ray explained. "Opening night. I'm writing up the show. Free publicity. Is it my fault the producers forgot to send me my comp tickets?"

Gavin watched Jem watch Ray. His voice was angrier as he said, "Your sort don't get comp tickets. Your sort—"

"My sort what?" Ray challenged. And then he focused on Jem. Their eyes met. Her cheeks flushed.

Gavin eyed her sideways like he would a rare delicacy. "She's striking when she dresses correctly, isn't she? When she isn't bounding about after lost pocket watches."

"Miss Watts would look striking in a burlap sack," Ray said as Jem blushed further.

Gavin smiled wickedly at Ray. He put his arm around Jem and lowered his lips to the tendrils of hair dangling over the creamy skin of her neck. "I've observed something that interests me, DeLuca. You never describe Miss Herringford in your pieces. As far as the reader knows, she is a store mannequin. But Miss Watts here? The *Hog* readership knows all about her graceful curves and blue eyes. I wonder why that is."

Even in the dim light, Jem could see Ray's cheeks flushing. Gavin smirked and pulled Jem back the way they'd come. "Come, Jem. That muckraking Italian's a menace," he said, "and we have a tour to get on with," he said. His hand found the small of her back again.

The three stood a moment, Jem's arms crossed over her waist, Gavin watching her, and Ray watching both of them with a question in his eyes.

"Mr. Crawley." The heavy curtain pulled open and a messenger stepped forward. "Your man said you might be back here. You're needed on urgent business, sir." He handed Gavin his second memo of the night.

Gavin's face darkened as he read it. "I have to go, Jemima." He dug into his pocket and placed some bills in her hand. "Take a taxi and I'll call 'round in the morning." He tilted her chin, kissed her cheek possessively, and strode away.

Jem bit her lip and looked at the money in her hand.

"Crawley's a cad," Ray said. "But you already know that. He left you at the drop of a hat without an escort in the back of a very dark theatre with a strange man."

"Not a strange man, Ray. Just you."

"And no tour."

"Ah, well," Jem picked up her skirt and began to walk toward the stage door and the exit.

Ray walked with her. "Now Crawley won't be showing you off to the actors and waxing eloquent about his patronage."

Jem soured slightly. "I hope the whole thing ends soon."

"You don't have to bait Crawley, you know."

"I'm safe enough."

"He treats you horribly. Perhaps I could give you a tour."

"You?"

"Upstairs."

"There upstairs?" Jem inclined her head.

"Jem, this is a double-decker. Did you know that?"

"What does that mean?"

"There is another theatre on top. A new one. Not even used yet. Tertius Montague modeled it after the best theatres in Chicago and New York. They are all doing it these days."

Ray led her out from backstage but, unlike Gavin, he didn't step behind her or press his hand into her back. His hands stayed in his pockets and he strolled several paces ahead. He gestured toward a side door beyond the exit to the street and propped it open for her. "There are those pretty new lifts in the foyer. But 'my sort' takes the fire escape." They stepped into the murky darkness of Victoria Street.

Jem hiked her skirts up, not trusting her hem against the rattling metal as they climbed. "Did you really watch the show from the rafters?"

Ray let her ascend first. "Best seat in the house. You see down on the top of the actors' heads. The music is just as beautiful, and you can see maybe the first two or three rows of the audience in their silks and feathers."

"Do they catch you often?"

"No one's beat me off with a broomstick yet."

When they reached the top of the fire escape, Ray instructed Jem to push the door open. Inside was darkness. She stayed near him.

He gently gripped her elbow. "The wonderful thing about Toronto, Jemima, is that there is always something hidden. It's all tunnels and trap doors and hidden stories." He reached into his pocket for a matchbox and located a discarded lantern. He flicked the match and lit the lantern. A stream of light filled the dark bower.

"Close your eyes," Ray said.

She shut her eyes and let him guide her forward. She heard the click of a light switch, and she could sense that the room around her had become brighter.

"Now, open up."

A secret garden fairyland surrounded her. Overhead, a forest of plants, vines, and leaves intertwined. The walls were elaborately painted in woodland splendor and vines hung from the ceiling. The colored lanterns specked the ceiling like a rainbow of stars.

"It's beautiful," Jem breathed. She ran her fingers over the intricate detailing and park benches rimming the back of the theatre.

"Its grand opening is set soon. Montague says he wants anyone who cannot leave the city in winter to have summer brought to them."

"Can you imagine?" She spun and looked at Ray. "You sit here and you feel like you are in a garden. The world has disappeared." She held out her hand, deftly tracing the outline of a gold-embossed design twirling around a pillar that was sculpted like a tree. It soared up to a painted night sky. "I had no idea this was up here. I pass the theatre every day on my way to work and never knew this was inside." She stood so close to Ray that their shoulders brushed. "It makes me want a garden."

He lingered there, their shoulders touching. "And what would you do with your garden?"

"I would plant all sorts of wonderful things."

"You'd need a..." he stumbled for the word. "A house that is green."

"Greenhouse." She smiled. "A greenhouse to incubate the flowers in winters. Yes. I would build a swing and sit on it and sip lemonade and watch the birds."

"Would anyone sit with you? Gavin Crawley, perhaps?"

Jem's neck was suddenly warm under her collar. "You know that's just a ruse."

"Do I?"

"Y-yes! Merinda has me going out and—"

"Didn't look much like a ruse tonight."

"What's that supposed to mean?"

"I could see you! Before the curtain even lifted, smiling into him. You're a better actress than the ladies onstage."

"Did you come here tonight to write up the opera or did you come to spy on me?"

"I don't trust that man. And you shouldn't either."

"I don't!"

"But you allow him all sorts of liberties, Jem. Why didn't you pull away?"

"You're angry with me?" Her eyes went wide. "Are you jealous?"

"You can admit you're attracted to Gavin Crawley, Jem. Handsome, well-dressed. Makes a lot of sense that a girl like you would fall for a guy like him."

Jem Watts falling for Gavin Crawley? Didn't he know? How daft could Ray be? Here she thought she was being so obvious, unable to keep her eyes from drinking in his profile. Unable to stop her hands from trembling whenever he spoke.

Gavin Crawley, indeed! She'd just have to do something to prove that...that...She thought a moment. Wouldn't the romantic buoyancy and winsome spirit that propelled the heroines she read of in books into their lover's eager arms guide her next move?

She knew then she was going to kiss him. She just didn't fathom she would do it so poorly.

Ray was standing close—too close, he knew. But before he could step back Jem lunged toward him. She made to loop her arms around his neck and brush her fingers over his hairline, perhaps expecting her lips to softly meet his. But what she actually did was topple and trip, and her nose found the hardest part of his shoulder blade.

"I'm so sorry!" But Jem seemed committed now. Winding deeper into a whirlwind of disaster and flailing arms, she steadied herself and pulled his face toward hers. Now their movements were anything *but* synchronized, and as she moved in and he tried to hold her up, she misjudged the angle and her teeth smacked hard against his lips.

"Ow!" Ray felt his top lip for blood.

"Oh, Ray," she said, looking horrified. "I'm so sorry!"

The way she jutted her chin up just made her the more vulnerable. The lace licking her throat and wrists had his skin prickling, and his brain wondered what a sudden friction of fabric-on-fabric might feel like. For a split second, his face slightly ducked toward hers, and he thought of parting her lips, cupping her face, and giving wholly in. Every nerve and tendon in him wanted to. She obviously wanted him to.

Instead, he put a finger to his bruised lip and pushed her to arm's length.

If Jem were any other girl…But she wasn't any other girl. She was a treasure to him. So purely, delightfully inquisitive. So wide-eyed and hopeful. No, Ray would as soon throw himself through the window as take advantage of her.

But Jem had a different idea. The bold little thing tried again, nearly bowling him over. He couldn't decide whether to catch her in his arms and kiss her properly or scold her. He settled on holding her gently but firmly by the arms and smiling sadly, despite the pain in his lip and nose. "No, Jem. Such a bad idea."

Her eyes got even bigger somehow and her face flushed.

"Jemima, you kissed me. Or tried to kiss me."

"I thought you might want some bold gesture. I thought that's what a girl's got to do to...to..."

Ray shushed her more harshly than he meant to, and then he rubbed his neck and exhaled. His lip really hurt. She looked so mortified. He touched her elbow gently. "*Spirito.* You've got it in spades, Jem. Courage too. You're a brave, crazy girl."

"Oh, you must think I'm a stupid fool."

"I like you better now than I did five minutes ago. Come, let's get you a taxi with some of that money Gavin Crawley's left you."

Moments later, they were at the base of the fire escape. The moonlight mingled with the electric lights spilling into the alley from Yonge Street.

"I've never done that before," Jem said.

"Thrown yourself at a strange man in a theatre?" There was a lightness in his voice.

She wouldn't meet his eyes. "Kissed anyone."

"Well, we can't count that." Ray shook his head. "Jem, your first kiss should be something wonderful. In a garden—a real one—with butterflies and someone who truly loves you. I..." He looked away. "Don't waste that on me."

They reached the end of the alley. Ray flagged a cab and it swooshed over, its veneer catching the lights of the electric marquis.

Ray beheld the contradictions in this porcelain beauty beside him. She didn't mind crossing way over the lines of propriety in so many ways, and yet she was as traditional as a Sunday School lesson in others.

He didn't want to look at her because he knew he'd hate the disappointment he saw there. But he didn't want her thinking he was cross, so he opened the door for her and pressed on a half-smile. "Good night, Miss Watts. Thank you for the tour." He raised her hand to his lips and kissed it. But he didn't look at her face. If their eyes met, he was sure she'd see everything, so he gazed at his shoes until the cab drove away.

Chapter Fifteen

For what is religion if not a great mystery? It is nothing if not a series of clues, a key to unlocking the greatest secrets of the universe. The careful detective will spend as much time pondering the spiritual mysteries as he does on whatever singular problem has crossed his path on any given day.

Guide to the Criminal and Commonplace, M.C. Wheaton

Crime doesn't stop just because one's mind is overtaken by the shame of a stolen kiss. Something M.C. Wheaton *should* have written, Jem decided. She could barely keep her mind still as she walked to Spenser's the next morning. Disappointment, absolute mortification, excitement—every emotion known to man seemed to be whirling through her.

Act normal, act normal, she told herself as she walked through the heavy doors to the mailroom. She coaxed her lips into a smile as she greeted the other girls, and she settled herself at her desk, hoping for something to jolt her out of this hopeless, purposeless daydreaming.

And just then, something did. The jolt came in the form of Tippy. She was sullen and pale, with burdened movements and bright eyes bereft of any sparkle or light. Jem was certain it was due to more than those notes she had presented to them, especially since those had seemed to stop.

Jem started staying later at Spenser's.

"Time to go, Jem," said Tippy on Monday afternoon as the clock ticked past five o'clock.

"Oh, I don't know. I thought I would try this conscientious thing." Jem winked at Tippy. "You're always being the model employee, so I thought maybe I can coax a raise out of old Mr. Spenser someday, eh?"

Tippy went positively pale. What could be hiding behind Tippy's jerked movements and constant anxiety? And of course Jem remembered the fuss Tippy had made on the street the other night. Jem needed to get Tippy out of there.

"How awful of me, Tippy," she lied. "My mind is a sieve. Miss Rumsfield in shipping asked if you would bring over those boxes by the end of day. Would you mind terribly?"

Once she had their corner of the mailroom to herself, she searched through Tippy's workstation. Tippy was a master at creasing the lines of brown paper and affixing floral garlands and other touches of her craft. It almost pained Jem to rip open the package that had been set slightly aside from the others and marked with the slightest black dot.

Beneath the tissue and decoration, Jem found a bound stack of papers. She leafed through them, her eyes wide. IOUs. Bets. And unless she missed her guess, it looked like the next race at the Danforth Tracks was going to be rigged.

"What a colossal waste of time," said Merinda, shrugging into her coat. "We come all the way out here and spend the whole evening at a ridiculous dance hall, and do you think the Morality Squad bothers to show their faces?" She grunted. "This is supposed to be Forbes's hunting ground." She re-balanced the weight from one uncomfortable foot to the other.

"At least everyone else is having fun," scowled Jem, taking one last look around the hall. Dozens of women loitered there, hazed with wine and without the protection of a beau, hoping for a stolen kiss or a frantic spin around the dance floor to some forbidden ragtime tune.

Instead of dancing, Jem had nursed a cup of punch and wondered why it was so easy for other girls to fall into the natural rhythm and grace of their partners' lead while she couldn't even muster up enough feminine prowess to land a decent first kiss.

Finally, having seen neither hide nor hair of the Morality Squad, they left.

Jem's heels pinched her. She pulled her gossamer wrap more tightly around her neck, suddenly conscious of the lateness of the hour.

"We're out here without an escort," Jem said, looking around warily.

"We're *always* out without an escort." Merinda's eyes were straight ahead.

"Never without hats and trousers. We're women tonight, Merinda. We're conspicuous."

Jem felt a sudden jerk of movement, and she heard Merinda scream. Jem's shoulder felt like it was being wrenched out of its socket as she was dragged into an alleyway, a broad hand over her mouth. Merinda was in the shadows, shoving her way forward and lashing out heatedly against her captor.

"Looking for me?" Forbes's voice was a gravelly grunt.

"Let her go!" Merinda reached into her purse and extracted her file, which she brandished like a small knife.

Forbes merely laughed and let Jem wriggle a little, his arm held tightly across her chest. "I've got a hundred pounds on you, lady. Gonna give me a paper cut with that?"

"What do you want? Money? I don't have my change purse here but—"

"You're a nuisance." Forbes looked from Merinda to Jem and back to Merinda again. "This little lady friend of yours is suspected of vagrancy."

Merinda rolled her eyes. "This is almost ironic. So much for tracking Forbes down for questioning."

"Mr. Forbes," Jem said in a voice that—much as she tried to imbue it with strength—could only be described as mouse-like, "we would like to verify that you are working for Mr. Montague. Further, that you are somehow involved in the Corktown Murders. Would you care to c-comment?"

Forbes spun Jem around and slapped her across the mouth.

Jem tasted blood. Her head went fuzzy and her sight momentarily blurred.

Forbes snarled. "It's a jail cell for you two. Roaming around, bold as brass."

Merinda lunged at him. She was wiry and quick, but Forbes pinned Jem with one arm and shoved Merinda backward with the other. She fell against the brick wall behind her with a thud.

"Merinda!" Jem shouted.

Dazed, Merinda adjusted herself, felt around her on the ground for her file, and determinedly rose again. By now, Jem was crying and hiccupping. She didn't like Forbes's smell of tweed and sweat and meat or his grimy palm over her mouth.

"So this is the Morality Squad!" Merinda was red-faced and disheveled, but she laughed without mirth. "Brutally assaulting women in the name of Montague's campaign?" She was enflamed. "I've got a few words for your judge."

"I've been watching you." Forbes looked at Merinda. "Lady detective in there with—"

"Spare me. Let Jem go." Merinda spread her arms. "Take me instead."

Jem tried to protest, but all she heard were the mumbled sounds of her voice filtered through Forbes's hand. In a rare moment of strength, she opened her mouth and bit down on his thumb with all her might.

Forbes let out a holler and Merinda flew at him, piercing his shoulder with her file and pushing him away. She grabbed Jem's wrist and spun her out of the alleyway and back onto the street.

Forbes might have had a hundred pounds on them, but they were faster. They wrestled out of their icepick heels and laces and were thereby able to speed up. Jem's hair whipped around her face as her carefully constructed hairstyle came unpinned, and she pushed it out of her eyes. She could hear the grunting Forbes picking up pace behind them.

"This was," Merinda said breathlessly as they ran, "perhaps a...poorly planned evening."

Jem stole a look over her shoulder. Forbes was gaining on them, holding his injured shoulder.

They reached the safety of Yonge Street and its bright lights just ahead of him. Despite the hour, the street was populated with patrons emerging from late suppers and cabs picking up their last fare of the night.

Merinda pulled Jem under a suitmaker's awning and they caught their breath, standing like sardines against the wall. Merinda peeked outward far enough to see their pursuer. He was searching the crowd, and Jem prayed he would look the other way.

He didn't.

"Well," Forbes said, approaching them out of breath and with rumpled clothes and tousled hair. "Not so ladylike now?"

"And we were ladylike before?" Merinda spat with a pointed look at his wounded shoulder.

Forbes yanked them out of the covering and onto the street, his grip bruising Jem's elbow. As Merinda was on the other side of his bulky frame, she couldn't lock eyes with her companion. They tripped along at his stride.

"Say there," a thin man said, stepping away from his lady companion to confront Forbes. "What is the meaning of this? What are you doing with—"

"Back to your silver spoon, mate," Forbes said with a snarl. "Morality Squad business."

The man's eyebrows rose and he evaluated Jem and Merinda afresh. Their red faces and tousled hair betrayed them. "I see," he said. "Well, if you're sure..."

Forbes yanked the girls along the street. A few other passersby noticed them, but they all seemed to reach the same conclusion. This citizen was in his jurisdictive right, their faces seemed to say.

"Is this really about our being at the dance hall?" Merinda asked.

"What do you think?" Forbes seemed to be enjoying the height he had over them.

"You hit her!" Merinda accused, wanting to jab him somehow.

"You stabbed me!"

Jem's face was flushed red and a bruise pricked on her cheek from the force of his hand. She kept her eyes on her feet. If they ended up detained, fine, she thought. The sooner the better. That at least would be better than being promenaded down Yonge, injured and tired, at the whim of this brute's every muscle-tugging move.

"Hello, Forbes," said a man in a heavily accented voice that drove Jem and Merinda's eyes immediately upward to make out Ray under a street light. "Got a quote for the *Hog*?" Ray readied a pencil over his notebook.

"I found these two unescorted females..." Forbes grunted.

"Misses Herringford and Watts." Ray inclined his head cordially. "Warm evening, is it not?"

Forbes was distracted and his grip slackened. Jem took the opportunity to rub the spot.

Ray watched and his face darkened, his eyes narrowing in on the side of Jem's mouth. "Roughing up innocent ladies, Forbes?"

"These two? Not innocent."

Ray folded his arms across his chest. "The longer you hold them there, the more time I'll have to figure out who put you up to this."

"The Morality Squad."

"Rubbish."

"I'm doing my job. I'm seeing them to Station One."

"For what?" Ray asked, pencil poised. "Walking?"

"This one," Forbes jutted his jaw at Merinda, "was making forward gestures at a dance hall. This one too." Forbes leaned over Jem. Her lip trembled and she shied back.

Ray chuckled darkly. "Yes, she's obviously the worst sort of criminal. You can tell by the whimpering. I'll tell my readers how expert you are at assaulting women."

Forbes grinned and nodded at Jem. "She's a pretty little piece, isn't she? Wouldn't mind holing her up in a cell for the night." His smirk gave away his meaning.

Forbes didn't have time to react before Ray closed the space between him and drove his fist deep into the fellow's nose. Forbes, twice the size of Ray, buckled back with the force. Merinda, impressed, dashed out of the way, pulling stone-still Jem with her.

"You will not speak of a lady like that," Ray was hissing.

"Don't be out alone at night," Forbes finally said, lamely, holding his palm to his nose and looking between the girls before turning and heading into the night.

Jem's knees nearly gave way under a wave of relief. She hugged her arms around her chest, shivering.

Merinda put her arm around her and pulled her in. "All right there, Jem?" She examined the side of Jem's face.

"I'll be fine." Jem's mouth shook. She didn't want Ray to see her cry.

Ray stepped closer. "You're pretty foolish, Merinda."

"I know." Merinda sounded almost guilty. Their eyes locked a moment and faced off.

Then he turned to Jem: "And you." He said it softly, but Jem ducked her head ashamedly. He reached an ink-stamped thumb and forefinger to her face and tipped her chin up. "Let me see." He stepped back, eyes still on Jem. There was blood on his knuckle.

"Well," Merinda said, sounding like herself again, "you're a rare breed of scrapping gentleman, aren't you, DeLuca?" She whistled. "Come with us. Let's see if Mrs. Malone can rustle up some lemon curd so we can thank you properly."

"I was on my way somewhere," Ray said distractedly.

"You just saved us from jail!" Jem's voice was tremulous. "We should repay you."

Ray didn't seem to hear her. Instead, he motioned for a cab. "Taking a taxi would have saved us all a lot of trouble tonight." He opened the door and motioned for Jem and Merinda to get into the backseat. Then he shut the door and strode away.

Reverend Ethan Talbot and Ray DeLuca met once a week at the St. James parsonage. They spoke of everything from the weather to poetry to whatever questions were plaguing Ray that week.

Though it was dark and he'd just put Jem and Merinda in a cab, Ray was on his way to one of these meetings. He picked up speed down Yonge and cut across Victoria and Court Street until St. James was in view. He strode past the cathedral and went instead to the manse. There, he thrummed the doorknocker several times until the housekeeper appeared.

She summoned her employer, and a few moments later Reverend Talbot joined him. "I was wondering where you had gotten to," he said with a smile.

"I'm sorry."

Talbot ordered tea and then motioned for Ray to follow him into his study.

Ray stared at his hands. "I came to ask your advice."

Ethan folded his hands over his desk. "And I am willing to listen."

Ray exhibited his bloody knuckles and related the story of his evening. "I feel that my writing—my articles—have endangered these girls. I've been their biggest advocate, but all I've managed to do is draw attention to them...and put them in harm's way." He shook his head. "They're women. They may stomp about in pants, and Merinda has some sort of stick she uses as a weapon. But none of it matters, none of their spirit or courage. You should have seen them in the arms of that brute. They were like twigs ready to break when pitted against a big man like Forbes." Ray looked down. "I don't want them to get hurt."

Reverend Talbot nodded. "You allowed them to be warriors. Women in the Bible didn't sit at home braiding mats for the men in battle. They went to battle too. Look at Deborah. Look at Esther."

Ray studied his hands. "But they couldn't fight this battle. So I interceded and punched a man in the face."

"You've a temper, Ray. I know that much from our time together." Ethan Talbot plucked off his spectacles, polished them on his shirt, and replaced them. "You see your sister in every woman, Ray. It's a wonderful quality. You want to protect women. There's not just one way to do that. These girls are trying to advocate for the less fortunate in the best way they know how. But, like you, they are on the side of right."

"What do you mean?"

"I mean," said Ethan, "that once in a while you can stand back and let them fight their own battles."

Ray studied his hand, the knuckles swollen from hitting Forbes. "Your wife must think you're a radical," he said.

"Please," Ethan snorted. "Where do you think all my brilliant ideas come from?"

Chapter Sixteen

The greatest error a bachelor girl can make is in admitting feelings for a man. Act aloof and conservative. Send slight, mystifying hints to tempt him and, believe me, he will follow. There is nothing more crass than a woman in pursuit of a man. He must be the one to take the lead, and she must make him work to win her.

Dorothea Fairfax's Handbook to Bachelor Girlhood

You're in need of a little outing," Gavin proclaimed on Sunday after the service had ended.

"What did you have in mind?"

"Luncheon. Come."

They walked in a silence that was far from companionable to the Maple Tea room. Soon dishes were spread out over the white linen, boasting some of Jem's favorite foods. Gavin was more attentive than she had given him credit for.

When he reached his teacup to his lips, she remarked, "You're left-handed."

"You're just noticing this now?" he joshed.

"I always forget somehow," she said. That was one of the first things Sherlock Holmes would have noticed. She clearly wasn't as observant as a lady detective ought to be.

"My parents never forgot," Gavin said shortly. "They had me try to correct it. Even had a tutor come in and tie my left hand behind my back so I was forced to write and eat with my right hand."

"How horrible," Jem sympathized.

"Now I use both." He demonstrated, lifting a forkful of food with his right hand.

Soon, they had exhausted the conversation topics of Toronto politics and the night at the opera. Jem knew that Merinda wanted her to press further and ask about the Corktown Murders, but Jem couldn't help but feel guilty for stringing this poor man on, no matter what her friend's suspicions were. So she asked about his job, he persisted in teasing her about her gem-like eyes, and he leaned for a kiss that she easily refused. They were in public, after all.*

"Tell me more about your family," she said after a bit of a silence.

"You tell me about yours first." Gavin reclined in his chair.

"They disowned me," Jem said simply. "Respectable shopkeeper and his wife in London, none too pleased with a daughter unwed and following Merinda Herringford around while ignoring their list of proper suitors."

"Until I came along."

Jem tugged uncomfortably at the collar of her dress. "I suppose so."

When the outing finally drew to a close, Jem returned to King Street determined to make an adamant plea to be spared from spending time alone with Gavin any longer. But, upon arrival at King Street, she found Merinda occupied with their Baker Street Irregulars.

Kat and Mouse had plenty to report. Gavin's checkbook was full of missed payments and drafts of owed money. Merinda entrusted Kat and Mouse with trailing him to see where he'd turn up. The *Globe* was so busy with coverage of the election that Gavin was kept busy at official functions. But Merinda wasn't going to pass up the opportunity to throw back the curtain on how he spent his time when he wasn't in pursuit of his next story.

"The Danforth Races!" she announced to Jem early the next morning, as her friend affixed a brooch to her shirtwaist in the front hall

---

* This was a better excuse, she decided, than telling him her affections were for a reporter with ink-stained fingers and a crooked smile.

before setting out to work. "I'm going to find out everything I can. According to Kat and Mouse, Gavin is always either on his way there or coming from the track."

Jem looked Merinda over. She wasn't clad in trousers, but rather a plain, comfortable dress. "You can't go without an escort."

"I know! Which is why I have one." Merinda snapped her fingers. "Jasper!"

Jasper appeared, dressed in a dapper suit and red tie. "Do I look the part, Jem?" he asked.

"It's a bit too big," Jem observed, wondering where Merinda had located the getup. "But you look quite handsome, Jasper. Now, Merinda, women of Gavin Crawley's class do not go to the Danforth races in common tea dresses. If Jasper has to look the part, so do you."

Jem was quite aware of the ticking clock and her tardiness to her shift at Spenser's, but she nevertheless spirited Merinda upstairs and performed a sort of magic. Moments later, draped in lavender—both the scent and the color—and with a wide-brimmed hat tipped at a fashionable angle on her blonde head, Merinda entered the sitting room. Jasper fingered his tie and adjusted it, trying to disguise his approval of Merinda's appearance, to no avail.

"Oh, close your mouth, Jasper," ordered Merinda, narrowing her eyes at his gaping mouth. "You look like a fish."

Jem leaned in and kissed him on the cheek. "You look dashing, Jasper. But I must run." She grabbed her handbag and set out the door. "Good luck!" she called over her shoulder.

"Aha!" Merinda said to Jasper, alive with an idea. She scurried off to the kitchen and returned with pomade she had purchased in case such an occasion might arise.

Jasper looked at a pot of gel in her hands. "You cannot be serious!"

"Constable Jasper Forth has brought murderers to justice and cleaned up the streets of our most dastardly criminals, and yet he goes weak at a little pomade!"

"How did I let you talk me into this?"

"Eyes front." She slicked the sticky substance on to her palms.

Jasper was on edge: a cat threatened with a bath. Then, she counted: "One, two..." She didn't wait until *three* before running the goop through his hair and slicking it down.

Jasper blushed something fierce. "It's cold and slimy."

"One moment!" She took her sewing scissors and trimmed his hair at the back. "Good. Let's go."

Jasper positioned a straw boater atop his head and Merinda wrapped her shawl around Jem's dress, its sash tied several times around her waist. She surveyed Jasper: bowtie, pin-stripes, two-toned shoes, white carnation. They looked the part.

"Well, Pygmalion." Jasper took Merinda's arm. "Do you feel as ridiculous as I look?"

"Indeed."

Jasper had commissioned young Officer Jones to escort them. Despite Jasper's recent demotion, he retained many loyal colleagues ready to pounce at his signal.

Upon arrival, Jones opened the door of the automobile for Merinda and helped her step out. Jasper led Merinda across the lawn of the beautiful, gated structure, beyond which were the racetracks.

"Do you know anything about racing?" Jasper wondered, thoroughly enjoying the warmth of Merinda's arm in his own. He had accumulated quite a few minutes of that pleasure on this trip alone. Leaving the townhouse had given them nearly four minutes. Down King Street to meet Jones and the automobile, another four. Now again! Even through the gloves she wore, her touch sparked his arm under his too-big jacket.

"Absolutely nothing," Merinda admitted.

"I know a bit from a few cases. Shouldn't be too difficult to find out a bit more about Gavin Crawley, not if those notes and planners Kat and Mouse stole are testament to his enthusiasm for gambling."

"Mmm." Merinda was distracted with hoisting up her skirt to step over a muddy patch on the lawn.

"And if this all comes to a head, I hope you'll let the police take over."

"I hardly think that is going to happen, Jasper."

"We'll see." He smiled in spite of her tone. "This is nice, you know?"

"What is? Narrowing in on Gavin Crawley?"

"Spending time with you. Being on the King beat I haven't had any time for our Saturdays at the University labs."

"And I have been solving crimes."

"Yes, you have." Jasper was still counting the minutes of their physical touch. This slow stroll across the lawn had given them another two minutes, ticking deliciously to three. It helped that Merinda wanted to play the part of a lady at the races.

Inside the racetrack arena, they encountered a kaleidoscope of chaos and color, shuffled movements, shouts of disappointment, and fists thrust high in the air. The smell of cigar smoke mingled with sweat and alcohol. Merinda could hear the swift, frantic plod of hooves without having to look at the horses on the track. Like a chugging train, they barreled along with frantic energy.

Men behind caged grates, not unlike bank tellers, doled out bids and bets.

Jasper put a hand in the small of Merinda's back and was surprised when she didn't back away. This play-acting was marvelous, he decided. How long could he keep Merinda playing the part of doting and attentive female?

They stood silently, and hopefully inconspicuously, for a few moments. The rhythm of the bettors and races and socializing ebbed around them like the tide.

Merinda nudged Jasper. "Look!" she hissed. "Tony."

"Tony?"

"Tony Valari. DeLuca's brother-in-law." She tried to point inconspicuously. "And there's Forbes."

"Aha. Yes, I'm acquainted with Mr. Forbes." Jasper pulled her into the shadows. Beside Tony and Forbes lurked a small blond man with a broad forehead and elfin ears.

"Is it all here?" Elf Ears squeaked in Forbes's direction.

"Yes," Forbes grunted. "Mr. Crawley—"

"Mr. Crawley owes me three hundred dollars. This is not nearly enough."

Forbes grabbed the little man's lapel. "This is what you get today."

"I expect interest!"

Merinda and Jasper exchanged a look. Gavin was in financial trouble—this they had already deduced. But he was still playing bookies and skimping on debts? How did he keep Tony and Forbes on his side? How could he pay his lackies? How could he keep taking Jem out to the finest places?

Tony joined Forbes in leaning over Elf Ears. "You're not the only one he owes money to. He owes me."

Jasper and Merinda watched as Forbes counted bills out to Elf Ears. With the money in hand, Elf Ears walked to the cages and placed a bet. Tony and Forbes wandered to the bar.

Jasper and Merinda followed them. The lounge afforded a view of the tracks, and Merinda was fascinated by the voice of the commentator. His speedy lips hastily projected words, his voice at turns in peaks and plateaus, mirroring the furious pace of the horses.

"Stay here." Jasper walked to the bar and ordered a couple of lemonades. He got a clear look at Tony and Forbes and settled at the bar to wait for the drinks, and to listen.

"He owes so many people," Tony said, his voice as heavily accented as DeLuca's.

Forbes nursed his whiskey. "Not my problem."

"If he can't pay them, how can he pay us?"

"You're right daft, aren't you, Valari?" Forbes smirked. "Montague. And he said he had something else up his sleeve."

The bartender brought the lemonades and Jasper was about to carry them off when Merinda joined him at the bar. They exchanged a look and tried to look disinterested, even as Forbes took a moment to swivel on his chair and overlook the nearly empty bar. Everyone else, it seemed, had opted to sit in the sun and watch the horses under its bright rays.

"After the election," Forbes said snidely, "things will change. Montague owes them both a lot of money. It's a bet. Just like this one," he said, indicating the racetrack. "Montague owes Crawley for keeping his stupid Morality Squad in the *Globe* and the Corktown Murders out. He knew the bad press from those murders could turn the tide of the election for him."

"I don't understand," said Tony.

Forbes sighed. "Horace Milbrook has decided his first order of business is to clean up hygiene in the Ward. That means no more of Montague's ramshackle housing, like St. Joseph's. Then, he is going to come down on illegal working conditions. Make sure workers in the garment factories and such are paid decent wages. Spenser and the rest of the city businessmen need Montague to stay in office if they don't want to lose a lot of money on those immigrants' paychecks."

Merinda and Jasper couldn't believe their ears.

"But you haven't been paid and I haven't been paid," Tony said. "I am getting a little tired of doing work with only the *promise* of future payment." He shook his head. "There are other ways to get money besides just waiting on the city's bigwigs."

Before Merinda and Jasper could hear what those other ways would be, Tony and Forbes left, perhaps to place another bet against money still owed to them.

Merinda and Jasper had heard enough. As they crossed over the soft green grass again, Jasper kept his arm looped with Merinda's. How many moments had he won now? Touching her arm gently. Pulling her close. Happily keeping his chin from colliding with her hat.

"You're in a lovely mood today, Jasper," Merinda said.

"I am! Beautiful day! Something to report on the criminal activity of Crawley, Forbes, and Tony." Not to mention something on the order of thirty minutes of physical contact with Merinda. "When I bring this information to the station, they'll let me off probation early! And to think, I didn't really have to do anything but sip lemonade with you at the races!"

"About that…"

"I might even get a promotion once they finally nab them. They won't make it halfway to Chicago. Why, I might—"

"You can't tell anyone, Jasper!"

He stopped. "Pardon me?"

"*I* need to solve this, Jasper. I know Gavin is linked to the Corktown Murders. Jem and I are *this* close."

"It doesn't work like that, Merinda. Two girls can't wipe out a city's worth of crime. The operation that Crawley is running has some major players in its ring. This is about more than two dead Irish girls. This is at the heart of our political system. It has ramifications for all of our citizens. Some of our leading men. If—"

"I know! I know! Using cheap labor and farming out thugs." She grabbed tightly to his arm and stared up into his wide blue eyes. "Jasper, I know you won't deny me this."

"You're not playing fair! You know how I…Well, you know—"

"I know you can't say no to me. Especially when I look up at you and bat my eyelashes." She batted them playfully.

Jasper tried to be cross with her. He shut his eyes so he wouldn't watch those eyelashes. But even with his eyes closed, a smile snuck out, and he knew Merinda Herringford was going to get her way.

Chapter Seventeen

Carefully designed to mirror the elegant world-class theatres in New York and Chicago, Tertius Montague is happy to have personally financed the grand Winter Garden Theatre. An invitation-only gala tonight will give Toronto's finest their first peek into what Montague and his designers assure us is a breathtaking whiff of a summer garden, even as the winter drags on.

The Hogtown Herald

hat are you doing?"

Merinda looked up from her desk as Jem entered, divesting herself of her damp coat and stomping her boots to rid them of snow.

"Nothing much," Merinda said. She picked up the notecard on which she'd been writing and leaned back, blowing on it to dry the ink.

Jem walked over and leaned over Merinda's shoulder, squinting to see what was written on the card. "Request the honor of your presence...grand opening...Winter Garden Theatre...*Martina* Forth! Merinda! Who's Martina?"

"I am," Merinda said matter-of-factly. "You've weaseled your way into the event on Golden Boy Crawley's arm, but I'm not letting you go on your own."

"So how..."

"This is Jasper's father's invitation," Merinda said with a roll of her eyes. "Honestly, Jem, you can be such a simpleton sometimes. Mr.

Forth is infirm, and he was all too pleased to part with his invitation. It's a simple matter to change *Martin* to *Martina*."

"I can see that," Jem said sarcastically.

Thereafter followed an hour of frenzied preparation, in which Merinda put on a yellow gauzy dress frilled with lace and Jem dressed in a similar one in blue. As Jem powdered her nose, Merinda tucked an ivory-handled pistol into her handbag.

The electric lights of Yonge winked at them alluringly. Even as they stepped off the streetcar, Jem could see the marquis of the theatre, far larger than its predecessor, attracting them from a block away.

The entrance to the theatre was bright and beautiful. On either side of the grand foyer the names of great composers and playwrights were ensconced in marble. A staircase led up to French doors with polished handles. They passed inside and followed the queue to the left of the golden lifts that would propel them to the second floor and the Winter Garden Theatre. The flash and pop of several cameras met them— Skip McCoy's among them. He spotted them, waved, and moved his way across the red carpeted foyer. "Miss Herringford! Miss Watts!"

"Quite a crowd, Skip!" Merinda said, taking in the whirlwind of music and laughter.

"This place has a secret, you know." He looked between them.

"A ghost?" wondered Merinda.

"A tunnel. Did you know there's a tunnel that goes straight under here, and all the way under the Dominion Bank, and comes out at Massey Hall?"

"Whatever for?" asked Jem.

"Something to do with the War of 1812. In case there was a siege or something. I always think of it, though. Whenever I'm here."

He continued on about its dimensions but Merinda, bored, shuffled Jem away, leaving Skip talking to himself.

Merinda and Jem merged with the throng in the foyer. Waiters rotated in a glistening carousel of poised silver trays and crystal champagne flutes. At the heart of the crowd, they spotted Henry Tipton, chief of police, clinking glasses with Tertius Montague.

"It's stuffy and boring here," Merinda complained. Her eyes danced around the room for something exciting. She swiped two flutes of champagne from a waiter and handed one to Jem.

"Misses Herringford and Watts, the city's favorite bachelor girl detectives." Gavin Crawley said it loudly and a few onlookers inched closer.

Jem blushed. Merinda laughed. Jem had no idea they had attracted the following they had. It would appear that Ray's articles in the *Hog* enjoyed several readers among the affluent. He'd be thrilled.

"Mr. Crawley, how pleasant." Jem responded with false sincerity as the crowd fringed back into their conversations and Gavin lifted Jem's hand to his lips. Jem still wasn't sure how to talk to him. How had she let Merinda let her get in this deeply? She looked to her friend for support, but Merinda was sipping champagne.

"When Tertius Montague is duly elected," Gavin said, raising his voice so as to keep those near within hearing, "he will assure that all females—all who would be so inclined—are kept from defacing the city's moral code with their ridiculous antics. Especially"—and here he narrowed his eyes at Merinda—"those who try their hands at a man's job in a business they have no right to be in."

Merinda seethed. "You're courting this fool?" she said to Jem.

Jem shrugged sheepishly, wanting to remind Merinda for the umpteenth time that she had wanted to cut ties with the cad weeks ago.

"Jem," Gavin said, taking her hand and leading her toward the buffet, "you won't always need to dash after Merinda to earn your bread, you know. Nor will you need to be seen out in ridiculous men's clothing."

"What about the immigrant women? Are you going to help them too? You and Tertius Montague? And what about me, Gavin, who—"

"Shh. Jem. You're getting ahead of yourself. And," he said with disapproval, "sounding far too much like your friend."

"That's not such a bad thing, Gavin."

"It is to me."

How much longer would she have to play this game? "I don't think we've ever wanted the same things, Gavin. Not where it counts. I don't believe in what you've made for yourself, and I don't believe in the man you are backing."

"Montague is the future of the city, Jemima. He proved it in his last term."

"I disagree," said Jem. "He hasn't yet learned that the world is spinning out of his control and that he can't put walls in place to stall its progress."

"You want Toronto to be overrun by crime? Festering with an influx of out-of-work vagabonds?"

"Families," Jem corrected. "With children. Wanting something new."

Gavin took her hands and spun her to the side of the mirrored foyer. "Jem, you would see the way I do if only you would tear yourself away from that friend of yours. There is some fire in you that goes with that sweetness. You can make me a better man, and I can give you the life you want."

Jem's brain spun. The life she wanted? What did Gavin know of the life she wanted? "What life is that, Gavin?" Strauss and strawberries, monogrammed serviettes, her parents' approval. Matching dishes from the Spenser's catalogue.

"A few babies," he said. "A beautiful home. How about a garden to rival the Winter Garden here? A man to worship you." His eyes wandered over her. "Your friend wouldn't understand. You know, you *are* allowed to give up the life she has tied you into for your own self-preservation, Jem."

"Is this a proposal?"

Gavin took a sip of champagne. "Do you want it to be?"

Before she could respond, a man in coattails announced that Tertius Montague would now receive guests in the lobby. Gavin joined the surge in that direction, and Jem was able to slip away.

Ray shoved his hands deep into his pockets. Every sinew in him ached to cry out and reveal Mayor Montague for the fraud he was. Scratch that—the entire night was a fraud. Montague and his business cronies were out to save pennies at the expense of women like Viola and men like Lars. What a sham, this need for the flounces and fervor, the lights and the promenade. He kept his tirade to himself, though, and observed. Reporters observed. His eyes traveled around the room, and he saw faces familiar, faces new, and faces that looked a lot like...

Jem and Merinda. Seeing them here where they shouldn't be was like a phonograph skipping over the same portion of music again and again. A smile couldn't help but flicker up the side of his face. He assumed Jem had been given an invitation by Gavin, but he wondered how Merinda had gotten in.

Jem was talking to Gavin, her shoulders rising as Gavin leaned into her. She folded her arms, then, in a most unladylike way, even in a pretty blue dress. This was the opposite of the Jem who had thrown her arms around him and rammed her lips against his and blushed to high heaven.

Gavin may have had the pedigree and background Ray desired, but he didn't have the heart of Jem Watts.

Alexander Waverley, editor of the *Globe,* stood before the crowd and announced Mayor Tertius Montague. Ray looked over and around top hats and feathers for a glimpse.

"In just a few moments," Montague boomed in his tenor voice, "it will be my privilege to introduce the garden I have waiting for you. The Winter Garden Theatre."

Enthusiastic applause followed.

Montague proceeded to speak about the construction of the theatre and the tireless efforts of its workers. He made sure to mention how it rivaled similar structures in Chicago and New York. He reiterated how the Elgin spanned a full city block in length, testament to the city's cultural sophistication.

Despite his bold words, Ray thought the mayor appeared nervous. Montague brought his handkerchief up and wiped his brow. This intrigued Ray, who had never seen the mogul anything but supremely confident. Why would he be anxious now, when the city was all but crowning him with the laurels of victory—not only for the mayoral race but also for his contribution to the city's architectural endowment?

"The Winter Garden Theatre is the icing on the cake," Montague said, folding his handkerchief away. "The Elgin and the Winter Garden will be accessible to everyone. There will be discounted prices for Wednesday matinees and Sunday afternoons."

Even the rich of Toronto, in their sateen and starched collars, applauded this show of benevolence.

Waverley stepped forward again and instructed the crowd to enjoy the buffet and conversation for another hour before proceeding to the second floor for the unveiling of the Winter Garden Theatre.

Ray kept to the side of the foyer as the crowd milled about. Swishes of satin and lace whisked passed him and up the grand staircase. At the top of the stairs, a chamber quartet launched into a Boccherini piece.

Skip was soon at his side, working with the plate in his camera and hoisting the stand. "Got some good pictures tonight, Mr. DeLuca."

"Get some of Montague mingling, will you? In his element with all of this liquor and food."

Skip nodded and set off.

Ray heard a small voice calling his name. It was high-pitched and rather desperate. He turned and found a young woman standing before him.

"You're that fellow from the *Hog*."

"Yes." Ray noticed she wasn't dressed to the nines, as were the other patrons. He assumed she'd winnowed her way into the event somehow.

"My name is Tippy. I have information on Tertius Montague and Gavin Crawley that you might find interesting."

He leaned forward. "Why not go to the police?"

"They wouldn't listen to me."

Ray shrugged. "I suppose not. Then, why not come to my office? It can't have been easy to get inside this gala."

"It couldn't wait." Tippy replied.

He led her out of the grand foyer and out to the street. Halfway down Yonge they paused under a streetlight.

"At first, I thought he was legitimate," Tippy said. "Gavin. He was a reporter. I had seen his name in the paper. He promised me money and trinkets if I did a few things for him. He told me he was doing some work to uncover corruption in the mayor's office. A kind of undercover assignment. One night, after I'd started slipping envelopes for him, he took me to Grace Street for supper. A quiet place. Just us with candles and wine, and I actually thought he might propose."

Ray knew where this was going. He took off his hat and scratched the back of his head.

"He told me everything. His family history. His dire financial straits. He used the mailroom for bribes and to pay his bookies. I did it for him gladly. We had all been in a tough spot, and he was turning his world around. He was going to change the city with his paper. And he cared for me." She held her arms tight around herself, looking small. "Mr. DeLuca?"

"Yes?"

"You're not writing this down. Don't you want it for your paper?"

Ray would give his left arm to expose Gavin Crawley, but would he do it at the expense of exploiting this timid, shivering girl? "I have a good memory, Tippy."

"There were rumors from the shirtwaist factory—I'd go with the girls there to the dances sometimes—that he had walked out with a girl on Montague's staff. I followed him to the Policeman's Ball and there he was with Jem. Haven't seen him in weeks and he pops up with Jem Watts. Telling her things that he told me, probably. And I knew then…" Tippy grabbed Ray's sleeve. "It's pretty horrible hearing the words that you thought were just for you said to someone else."

Ray nodded. They stood in silence a moment. "You want me to use this information to ruin him?"

Tippy smiled sadly at her shoes. "Jem took me to see a moving picture show once. *Oliver Twist*. And in it there's this woman—Nancy—and she will do anything to protect her man. No matter how he treats her."

"And you're like that Nancy?"

"I don't want to be trapped by Gavin. He'll keep using the same words." She shook her head. "So you'll run this—all of this—in your paper? Destroy Gavin, Mr. DeLuca."

Ray thought a moment. "The worst he can do is maybe make you lose your job. But he can't do that without exposing himself as the one who had been using you at Spenser's. Is there more you're not telling me, Tippy?

"I…can't."

"Then there's little I can do for you other than make sure you get to the trolley." He took Tippy's arm and steered her toward Agnes Street. They walked in silence, Ray keeping a slight grip on her elbow. He was thinking over her words—apparently to such a distracted degree that he didn't notice the footprints closing in behind him until they were very near.

Ray looked over his shoulder and cursed in Italian. "Tony, go home."

"Can't do that, Ray."

Forbes stepped out of a shadow to join Tony.

"Tony, you keep the worst company," Ray said. "Streetcar is right there, miss." Ray inclined his head and motioned for Tippy to leave. Tippy looked unsure. Tony and Forbes settled their eyes on her, and something in Ray's chest jumped. "Tippy, please go."

Tippy turned to leave.

Forbes grabbed her arm. "You've got it all wrong, DeLuca. We're not here to see you at all."

"Pity," Ray said sardonically.

Tony edged in. "We're here to see this young lady. If you'll kindly get on with your business."

"Tippy," Ray said, widening his stance slightly, "you seem to already know Mr. Forbes here. Allow me to present Tony Valari, my brother-in-law and father to my little nephew, Luca. For whom he daily sets a shining example."

"*Silenzio,* Ray!"

Forbes tightened his grip on Tippy. "Come on, young lady."

Ray felt ill. "Oh, don't start this again. Does your nose need another adjustment, Forbes?"

"This has nothing to do with you!" Forbes grabbed Ray's lapel with his free hand. "I haven't forgotten, DeLuca."

Ray wished for a nice, quiet hole to sink into.

"Problem here?"

They all four turned at the rap of a stick and the sudden appearance of a constable in hat and regalia.

"Constable Forth!" Ray's relief was audible in his voice.

Forbes let go of Ray.

Jasper's eyes narrowed at Tony and Forbes. "The Morality Squad is getting rather violent these days." Though not as bulky as Forbes, Jasper's height gave him the advantage.

Tony slipped away down the street. Forbes lingered, watching Jasper's stick thumping the pavement.

"Your friend has the right idea," Jasper said. "I suggest you also go about your business, Mr. Forbes."

"Just doing my duty, Constable." He spat the latter word. "Montague's orders."

"Montague is at that big soirée. So I am sure he won't mind your taking a break from your unbridled enthusiasm. Besides, it looks to me that this young lady was not without an escort, so you have no reason to detain her." Jasper thumped the ground a few more times.

With a growl at Jasper and Ray, Forbes turned and walked away.

"You all right, Ray?" Jasper asked kindly.

"Thanks to you."

"What about you, miss?" he asked Tippy.

The girl was stiff, except for a slight trembling in her hands. Perhaps she was imagining what could have happened had Ray and Jasper not been around.

Jasper extended the crook of his arm to her. "I'll see you safely home." With a quick smile to Ray he led Tippy off into the night.

Ray fell against a lamppost and caught his breath. Clearly, a girl could not end her association with Gavin Crawley that easily. His eyes flitted back in the direction of the Elgin Theatre, where light spilled over the sidewalk.

What did that mean for Jem?

He didn't want to think about it. He settled his bowler on his head, hoped that Skip would finish up for him, and set off in the direction of St. Joseph's.

Merinda looked around for DeLuca, but he had long since left. On the other side of the room, Jem was yawning. Merinda couldn't blame her: Crawley was insufferable company. Though she couldn't see him now and wondered if he had also left. Montague was making a falsely humble speech that was spilling over itself with a long list of his strengths.

Finally reunited, Jem told her that, no matter how it furthered their investigations, she could not stand another moment in Crawley's company, and she would entertain his advances no further. However, having seen the Winter Garden Theatre, she was adamant that they stay long enough for Merinda to steal a peek herself.

Merinda agreed on the condition that they wait out the rest of the Montague's speech in the vicinity of the refreshment table.

CHAPTER EIGHTEEN

The Hog has become my home. There's something comforting about the smell of wood shavings and fresh ink and pulp mingling with the hops and barley from the nearby distillers. In the summer, the seagulls caw while the ship's horns belch as they pass the rim of the harbor.

From a journal Jem has nearly committed to memory

Ray flicked the electric lights off. While most of the city's papers had had reliable electricity for at least a dozen years, in this respect as in all others, the *Hog* trailed behind. The lights buzzed and danced before finally extinguishing.

The sky was candy pink as he clicked the door behind him and hurried back to his bed at St. Joseph's. The last beams of sun were yawning over the roofs of the distilleries, and men outside St. Joe's were milling around. Ray spotted Lars on one side of the rickety porch, a notebook open on his lap. As Ray was meandering over to join him, he heard his name bellowed from the street. Ray and Lars looked up.

"Forbes," Ray said, "go away."

"Tony and I want to have a little chat. About last night."

Ray noticed Tony hovering beside a shrub nearby.

Lars looked confused.

Ray shrugged his shoulders at the big Swede. He slumped down the walkway and onto Elizabeth Street. "What do you want to talk about?

"You interrupted us."

"From accosting that poor girl?"

Forbes took Ray's collar. "You get in a lot of people's business, you know that?"

"Part of my trade," Ray said uneasily. He didn't like the grip Forbes had on him.

"Not anymore," Tony said, stepping into Ray's face. "Mr. Montague's tired of you—and your paper."

Ray could easily take Tony, but Forbes? Forbes was taller. Much taller. Ray, on the other hand, was faster.

Which was good, because at that moment, Tony reared back to deliver a punch. Ray slipped aside and set off down Elizabeth Street.

Ray only got as far as Agnes Street before Forbes caught up. He grabbed Ray and, in the same movement, drove his fist right into the stomach, taking his breath. The second was even harder, and Ray was sure it had broken a rib. Unable to peer beyond the fuzz in his eyes, Ray tried feebly to avoid more impacts. More blows fell, and one landed square on his jaw, rattling his teeth.

Then he was pushed back and someone stood over him. A blurry figure grappled with Forbes, ducking punches and landing blows of his own.

Ray tried to keep his eyes open. The world was spinning and sickly green. His breath spurted in chugs and gasps. There came a sound of a large body striking the ground hard, and with unfocused eyes he beheld a large man chasing off two smaller figures who looked a lot like Forbes and Tony.

Then that someone had an arm around Ray and was lifting him up.

Ray blinked at his savior. "Lars?" He felt the sticky blood at his temple and pressed a hand into his aching ribs.

Lars spoke in Swedish in sympathetic tones.

Ray assured him he was fine. He bent over to catch his breath, then he straightened as gingerly as he could. "Thank you, my friend. You really came through." He held onto Lars's arm a moment and coughed. Lars' eyes clouded with worry. "I'm fine. I just have to see someone. I'll see you later. Thank you again."

He fumbled in his pocket for a few bills and splurged for a cab ride. Lars helped him in and the cab drove off.

"Where to?" the driver asked, raising an eyebrow as he noted the blood on the side of his face. "Nearest hospital?"

"No." Ray couldn't go to his sister's, not with Tony lurking about. "Take me to 395 King Street West."

"Merinda, there is an unmarried man asleep in our house."

"It's not my fault he fell asleep," said Merinda, barely glancing up.

Jem had returned from the nickelodeon with Tippy, waltzed into the sitting room, and almost sat on poor, bloodied Ray. "I'm not moving him," Merinda continued. "Mrs. Malone was a fright having to wash him up and bandage him. I still think we should go to the doctor."

Jem looked over her shoulder and then shot Merinda a pleading glance.

"Mrs. Malone is here. And if you go to sleep, as I intend to do, then you'll forget and in the morning, at the breakfast table, in broad daylight, it won't seem so odd after all." Jem looked pained and unconvinced. "Jemima." Merinda's voice was firm. "He gave me some amazing insight on Tippy. I'm surprised he made it here at all. Forbes gave him quite a roughing up."

Jem winced. Was it possible, she thought, to feel someone else's pain?

Jem made to go up the stairs but found her feet weighted to the step. She heard Merinda run the faucet and begin her evening toilette. She inhaled a breath that she held until she felt lightheaded.

Invisible wheels turned in her head nearly as loudly as the grandfather clock tolling the late hour.

From the corner of her eye she spotted Ray's notebook on the desk.

She couldn't believe it sat there, exposed, with him slumbering closely nearby. Mrs. Malone had found it under her bed* and Jem had mumbled something about needing to keep it. Thus, it made its way to the front bureau. Her heart skipped in an irregular beat. She moved in its direction on tiptoe, watching carefully as the oil lamp flickered and danced, eerie shadows enlarging objects into towering monsters.

Jem often wondered as to Ray's age. In sleep, she could see his youthful face betrayed more years of life than she initially thought. A shadow beyond the dancing lamp hovered over his unshaven face, the stubble flecked with gray.

She inched closer. Mrs. Malone had tied a white bandage on his forehead. Jem watched his breath whisper across the pillow. She drank in that face, her favorite weakness. Jem balled her fists to fight the inkling pricking the ends of her fingertips. She'd always wondered what his thick, dark hair would feel like to her touch. Surely she had spent enough time over the last several months mulling on it—when he was hatless, or when its luster was restrained by his bowler, or under that tweed cap that took half a dozen years off his face.

Jem leaned forward, extended her arm, intent on a thought that would never cross the mind of a proper lady. She retreated. Then she took a deep breath and extended her slightly trembling fingers and...

It was thicker than she had imagined. The slightest flick of her fingers exposed gray underneath its ebony surface. Her nerves exploded. Was it just that she was taking liberty that made her flush to the tips of her ears, or was it that...that...?

She loved him. She had spent her whole life tripping over interactions with the opposite sex, but she never fathomed that it was because she hadn't met *him* yet. When God made a Jem, she was sure He must have made a Ray. She'd do anything for this man, she decided, still feeling the weight of his hair on her fingers even as she slowly backed away. She would sacrifice, even change or improve or refine.

---

* Perhaps not Jem's most inspired hiding spot.

Her hand, still tingling, fell at her side. She crossed her arms as her mind whizzed in a thousand directions at once, barreling ahead of her.

"You're thinking rather loudly, Jemima." There was a sly smile in Ray's sleepy voice.

Startled, Jem tripped back and dashed from the room, flurrying up the stairs and slamming her bedroom door behind her.

Ray's head throbbed something fierce but sleep wouldn't come to him again. He sat up and the room spun in the darkness. Outside he could hear the echoing clop of a horse's hooves. He picked up the lamp and washed the room with its buttery light. Vowing that anything he found in the bower of the bachelor girls would never make it into the pages of the *Hog*, Ray walked over to the window where the pale yellow light from the streetlamps was puddling on the pavement. He let the lace curtains rustle to rest. To his right was a chalkboard. He raised the lamp to it and connected the dots of its elaborate web. Articles had been pasted there, and ideas were scrawled in a sure, strong hand he was sure belonged to Merinda.

Many about Gavin Crawley. Many about his gambling debts. A lot familiar to him from the night after he and Merinda broke into the *Globe*. Ray's eyes fell from the board and to the bureau beside it. It was scattered with papers, missives, and telegrams. He tipped the lamp closer to make out writing. Some notes thanked the Ward detectives, while other notes were of a more housekeeping nature: lists and a budget in a much more feminine hand, most likely Jemima's. He fanned his fingers out and searched a little more, peeking over his shoulder to ensure that their housekeeper was still abed—that his exploration was not disrupting her slumber.

Then his fingers felt something so familiar it felt like it belonged in his hand. Its weight filled his palm, and with the sensation a cask of memory spilled open.

His journal.

She had lied to him. To *him!* Sojourned into the deepest thoughts he had. He was exposed. Not, he supposed, unlike a girl, sopping wet, trousers around her ankles outside a theatre.

The space of the room closed around him. His palm found the throbbing pulse of his injured head. Clutching the book tightly, he mazed back to the sofa and lowered himself gingerly. *The words....* He deftly thumbed through the pages, words springing and warmly reuniting him with his past...*All of them.*

The words: cajoling and crowded, pricking his skull and plucking his memory. She had held them all in her lavender-scented hands, internalized behind the chestnut fringe of her curls.

She knew it all.

He sat, delighted at reclaiming a part of himself, yet betrayed that his heart and poetry had been pried open.

His anger rose, flushing his face. He wrestled out of his coat and vest, repositioning himself on the sofa in his shirtsleeves, collar buttons open, wincing as his careless movements wreaked havoc on his ribs. Finally, in that strange moment wedged between deep night and the promise of hovering day, he drifted to sleep.

Morning came, peering through the window and spilling over the Persian carpet. Mrs. Malone followed with a pot of fresh water and a smile.

Ray rubbed his eyes. Opening them, he recalled why he was here, feeling the bandage at his head and, like a similar wound, found the notebook Jemima had taken.

He removed the blanket from his stretched frame and accepted coffee while declining breakfast. If he could escape with but a note to Merinda for her kindness and get out into the safe, sane day, he would do so. He didn't want to see Jem. He didn't want to see the flash of embarrassment on her pretty face, nor did he want to experience the temper he would fail to swallow down while he listened to her recant and give whatever explanation she would trip over for the book being in her possession.

Jem couldn't believe how stupid she had been to have kept the journal as long as she had, knowing full well Mrs. Malone's efficiency. Why the housekeeper was a downright busybody at times. She stared at her pale, sleep-deprived, worried-wracked face in her mirror and noted the purple moons under her blurry eyes. Her fingertips held a memory that her heart sped up to snatch and keep. She straightened her shoulders.

Finally, she tilted her chin and descended the staircase. Best dispel the strange looks and small talk before Merinda arrived.

Ray was at the bannister, slowly, painfully shrugging into his coat.

"You can't leave!" she told him. "You can't. You're not well enough. We'll ring Jasper to bring Jones by."

Ray turned, and the smile that met her was sardonic, while his eyes flashed fire: "I'm sorry, our housekeeper took your coat to launder," he imitated in sarcastic singsong while holding up his notebook.

The blood drained from Jem's face, throat, and all the way down to her toes. She gripped the bannister. "Oh."

"Why do you have this, Jemima?"

"I kept it." She watched him swallow, even as those coal eyes of his sparked. "I couldn't bear to give it back to you because I would miss it. And I thought a hundred times of how I would explain it to you, but…"

She inched closer. He stepped back. She closed in again. He was now nearly at the door, his hand reaching for the knob. The book was clutched possessively, but every part of him seemed magnetically drawn in her direction. Then, unexpectedly, his ink-stained fingers found their way in her hair. Close, her body unsure which sensation to follow, his fingers explored her loose, unkempt curls. He touched her cheek then. His finger trailed down her face, claiming her with words yet to be spoken.

She caught her breath as he stiffened and retreated.

"You shouldn't have kept this!" His voice was surly. "It means a lot to me and I thought I had lost it. Now you know everything. The bad, the horrible. You had no right."

"I..."

His hands found her wrists and gripped tightly. "Stop being ridiculous, Jemima." His eyes lingered over the open book of her face.

"I can't stop it!" Jem's voice was a stubborn sob. "I won't try."

When he spoke again, he made a concerted effort to even his voice to passionless and stale: "This is a silly schoolgirl fantasy. It's not worth it." He threw her arms down and crossed his own. His hands moved at a speed that matched his thoughts. "I don't want to hear you talk to me about this again. Do you hear me?" He tucked the notebook in his breast pocket and adjusted his bandage.

Jem knew she had taken a piece of him. Knew and wanted to safeguard it, even still. She wanted to act as keeper of his beautiful words. The vulnerable bits of their beautiful city that no one ever saw.

"You changed everything for me," she admitted tremulously, thinking of the way that his journal and his terrible poetry inspired her to walk the city streets as if viewing it for the first time. She would look up to note the ornamentation rimming every roof; she would look down and notice the homeless with their hands outstretched, the children lacing through the traffic, knee-high, attempting to beat each other at a game of tag. "I see everything differently now. I wake up and the city is new. I go to work and that is new too, and when Merinda and I go out and solve these little mysteries of ours...well, you're there too! I believe in everything you've ever written and everything you will ever say. Your thoughts are my thoughts. Don't you see?" She emboldened herself; erected her spine. "But I can't say them. I can't speak for those who can't speak for themselves. I am just a woman. But you..." she pointed at him. "You can tell the world. You can use those words of yours like a knife that cuts through everything that is unjust and horrible and you can make it right."

Ray was wise enough to read between her lines: "I couldn't take care of you. Even if I wanted to."

"I am not a girl who needs taking care of. I'm like you. I don't want anything else. Neither do you. Look at the way you're looking at me!"

"You and Merinda." He cursed in Italian. "I write you into these little columns and you make it out to be some...some..." He faltered into Italian again.

Jem took advantage of his search for words. "I love you!" she blurted. He must have known it! Everyone knew it, but his eyes flashed all the same. He shoved his hands in his pockets. All he found therein was a scratched and rusty old pocket watch. Nothing that would get more than a few dollars from the pawnbroker.

He held it up to her. "Here's my whole fortune, Jemima. Here's what you gain by telling me this." He turned the watch around. "A piece of junk and a whole lifetime of terrible mistakes to go with it."

He shoved the watch back in his pocket and grabbed her forearms tightly through her gossamer dressing gown.

"You're hurting me!" she said.

Ray flinched and though his grip slackened, he didn't let go. "Why did you have to tell me that?"

"I didn't say anything you didn't already know."

"You used the words." He turned to the door.

"Don't go away. Isn't there some way? Any way at all? Can you look me in the eye and tell me you don't love me? I always thought maybe you did."

Ray kept his eyes on his shoes while he listened to her heart break. "I will never regret using those words," she said. "Not to you. Not ever."

The door swooshed open. Then it clicked shut and she was left alone.

Chapter Nineteen

*To successfully draw a conclusion to any mystery, one
must have a solid plan. Scope out your perimeter, map
every moment, and prepare for the worst-case scenario.*

Guide to the Criminal and Commonplace, M.C. Wheaton

E lection Day. Ray twirled his pocket watch around his finger
as he watched the throngs outside the *Tely* office.

How impatiently they waited for election results. Men
leaned forward, bouncing on the balls of their feet. An invisible line
cut between the one set of reporters who were eager to hear that Horace Milbrook had taken the majority and another set who waited with
bated breath for the news that Tertius Montague would continue
his reign. Ray felt an affinity with those of the *Tely* and the *Star.* He
wanted to see Horace Milbrook have a chance to fulfill all the promise his campaign had predicted.

The doors opened and the *Tely* newsboys hoisted unfolded papers
off their shoulders. The ink was barely dry, the pulp and fibers still
warm, the energy of the reporters' rapid typing not yet a memory.
Men tripped over themselves, handed over their ready coin, and
snatched their slice of history.

Tertius Montague had won another term.

Ray rapped his knuckles on the door of Viola's house.

She appeared and smiled when she saw him. But then her eyes went to the scab on his forehead, and she reached up to touch it. "Did Tony do this?"

Ray winced. It still smarted a bit. "And that henchman Forbes."

Viola's nose wrinkled at the funny word *henchman*.

Ray followed her to the kitchen table. Luca was playing with a wooden train in the corner, and Ray stooped to ruffle his hair and kiss his forehead. Viola poured tea from a cracked pot and set out a plate of biscuits. Beside his plate was a small jar of lemon curd. He spooned out a large dollop and smiled for the first time in ages.

"Just like Nonna's."

"Yes. She taught me to make it," said Viola. "I remember stirring the pot with her, her big hand covering mine..." Her voice broke. "We had everything. Why did we come here?"

"No, we didn't have everything, Viola. The past does that. It lures you back and tricks you into thinking it was better than it was. The English word is *nostalgia*. It means a pain for home."

"Home pain." The words in English were mournful in her alto voice.

He took out his journal and opened it to the photograph pasted on the front flap.

"I forgot about this." Viola said, running her finger over the photograph's sepia browns and muddled yellows that couldn't keep the sun from shining alive on the print. His hand held Viola's in the scene, shoes hidden under tall grass whistling from a wind he could even now feel across his cheek.

"Home pain," he repeated, gently unpeeling the photograph and handing it to her. "You keep it."

She pressed it to her heart. "I want a home again, Ray." Her voice was barely a whisper. "I want a home. I don't want...this life for me and Luca." She tilted her head in her boy's direction. Luca was a little cherub playing on an heirloom quilt, one of the few things retained from their passage.

"Vi, I will always take care of you. Both of you. I will provide for you. Tony only takes. He takes from you and he hurts you and he takes you for granted."

"I love him."

Ray blew out a sigh of frustration. "You have to start loving yourself and Luca more, Vi. More than that shiftless, useless—"

"You have never been in love," she said in Italian. "You do not know. It is not that easy."

Ray wasn't ready to talk about love. Not after the words Jem had spoken. Not when the memory of that girl wouldn't leave his mind even for a moment. "Practice your English," he said lamely.

"No, you stop with this English. You always say that when you want me to talk about something other than the conversation we're having."

"You need to learn it so Luca can get by, so he can have a life here."

"I don't want a life here, Ray. I don't want to be here at all. Tony would never be in this trouble if we had stayed home. Never." She wrapped her arms around herself. "It is too cold here. No one wants us."

"There's nothing left for us in Italy. Nothing. You remember how it was, how hungry we…Everything is here. Our future is here." He reached for one of her hands. It was red and cracked from the cold, and her nails were chipped. "I will always take care of you. I will provide. But I need you to be strong so that…so I can have a life too."

A crease appeared in her forehead. "What do you mean?"

"Do you ever think I've wanted more too, Vi? But I've had to put you first. Put Luca first. Of course it's been my joy to do so, and I'll keep doing so, but sometimes I feel that I've delayed my own life so you could…" He stopped, and Viola's eyes flooded with tears.

She sobbed an apology that he could barely make out in any language.

"English, Vi."

"Ray, I've ruined your life. Like I've ruined Tony's and Luca's—"

Ray put a finger to her lips. "Shush. You have done nothing, my beautiful sister. You, with your good heart and your darling little boy.

I should not have said anything. I've used you as a barrier. I've put you in a position you didn't deserve to be in. My mind uses you as an excuse not to move forward with my life."

Viola looked puzzled.

Ray swallowed and tightened his grip on her hand. "I...I must try to understand myself."

"Good luck with that," she teased, a slow smile tickling her cheek.

He smiled in return. At first just a small one, but then it stretched wide.

"Il tuo sorriso è bello" she gushed, seeing his smile. "Nonna would melt in her chair."

The day started out innocently enough. After a sleepless night, Jem stepped into a shirtwaist and skirt, preparing for a shift at Spenser's. And while Merinda stayed behind studying her case files, Jemima stepped out into the city. Her city.

She got on the streetcar and watched the passing houses, mercantiles, milliners, and grocers. Then the broad, bright steeple of St. James came into view, and she stepped off the trolley, forsaking all thoughts of tardiness.

Jem climbed the steps and let the light filtering through the stained glass bathe her face. Then she sat in the empty sanctuary, watching the sun on the polished tiles, listening to the silence speaking all the languages in the world.

"Miss Jemima Watts."

Reverend Ethan Talbot was standing in front of her. She smiled at him, and he took a seat beside her. "Is something troubling you?"

"What makes you think that?" Jem asked.

"You don't usually grace us with your presence midweek. Off solving mysteries, usually. Or working at Spenser's."

"Do you think I'm very ridiculous?"

"Ridiculous?"

"Don't most respectable women have houses and families?"

Reverend Talbot smiled "Many of them do, don't they? But not all."

"I have a friend," she said, "who believes that all of life's questions seem to be answered here, within these very walls." She remembered the line scrawled in Ray's journal in his fine, slanting handwriting. "Do you think there are places where we can hear God more clearly than others?"

He shrugged. "Maybe. But God is going to speak to you no matter where you decide to meet Him." And he left her to her thoughts.

Silence. It was a funny thing, Jem thought, to finally realize where one stands, to peel back the curtains of wisdom from other sources, to supplant the Wheatons and Fairfaxes of the world with one's own ideas. She had a voice! She could speak! For others, surely, but also for herself. Merinda's voice may have cut more sharply, but Jem's passion matched it. Her integrity never wavered. She had a voice and she could make it heard.

The seamstresses did not speak. The Corktown Girls did not speak. Could not. Would not. Instead, they were fearful of words. But Jem would embrace words to honor them. To speak for those who were deprived of a voice.

She saw more clearly than she ever had.

Jem took her time getting to Spenser's, opting to wander. The energy she'd felt in the cathedral had mellowed to contentment. In her pocket she kept the well-creased note from her parents, received the morning they'd found the first dead Corktown girl. She kept it and its attached pamphlet of respectable activities near at all times. It was a crinkled emblem of something she had once been but would never be again.

She no longer cared about propriety. She no longer cared to be one of those girls who married at the proper age, who had their lives figured out, who wouldn't be caught dead in trousers. The girls who kept better company. A surge of her earlier giddiness returned, and she raised her fist to the sky. "Hallelujah!" she shouted to King Street, catching the eye of many passersby. Even more turned to look when she shouted, "I'm not going to be one of those girls!"

And since she wasn't going to be one of *those girls*, she could do exactly what she wanted. She could love whomever she wanted— even if he refused to love her in return! As for her parents' expectations and every young lady's etiquette guide, why, expectations be hanged. She pulled her parents' note from her pocket and kissed it with fond remembrance.

And promptly ripped it to smithereens and watched the tiny pieces float like wings on the air.

Ray sat back in his chair as Skip droned on about working for a better paper.

"After the election, I decided I don't want to be stuck here forever." He pushed his red hair back from his face. "I don't, Mr. DeLuca. I want to work at one of the papers people wind around the block to get a headline from."

Ray let him go on, hoping he would stop soon. He wanted to get this St. Joseph's piece in perfect shape before presenting it to McCormick for the next edition. He had stayed up all night working on it, eating the rest of Viola's jar of lemon curd, drinking the last dregs of coffee, convincing himself that his jumbled thoughts were a result of a story in action and not of Jem. He had his journal back but it sat untouched on the corner of his desk. He was convinced it still smelled of lavender.

When the door jangled open he was ready to hop up and show McCormick his working draft. But his boss's large shadow failed to appear. Rather, a slight girl dressed in ragged boys' clothes stood panting and red-cheeked in front of him.

"Which one are you?" asked Ray.

"Mouse."

"Right."

"I need you to send a telegram."

"And why would I do that?"

"Because it was faster to run here then to the west side of King Street and I just saw Mr. Crawley and Forbes put a sack over Jem Watts's head."

CHAPTER TWENTY

I beseech those tied up with rope to breathe slowly. The tighter and more rigid you become in your struggle, the deeper your bonds will cut. A survey of your perimeters and a quick, rational assessment of your circumstance, however dire, is the most prudent action.

Guide to the Criminal and Commonplace, M.C. Wheaton

I need someone with whom to share my golden moment," Merinda said into the telephone. She was in the sitting room staring at the ceiling, having spent the better part of the previous night and that morning working out every last detail of the case. Everything pointed to Gavin Crawley, as she had maintained since the beginning. But now she felt she had ironed out every wrinkle.

"What do you mean 'golden moment'?" Jasper asked. "And where's Jem?"

"She's gone out—had to work today. What matters is that she's gone, and I've solved everything, and I want you to come over so I can share my stunning deductions."

"Shouldn't you be calling the police?"

"You *are* the police."

She could hear his exasperation even over the telephone. "Merinda, must you continue this ridiculous and dangerous pursuit of a criminal?"

"I bought a revolver."

"Which you can't even shoot in target practice."

"Nonsense. I didn't purchase it to fire it. I just threaten and point. It startles a perpetrator and puts them ill at ease and—"

"Merinda, my lunch is getting cold."

"Well, eat fast and skip dessert and take a cab over here just as fast as you can."

"It's apple pie!"

"Constable Forth, with whom do your loyalties lie? Me, your dearest friend and most esteemed colleague in all things scientific and detection, or...or...*pie*?"

Less than twenty minutes later, Jasper was seated on Merinda's sofa. "So it's Gavin Crawley?"

Merinda nodded. "I should telephone DeLuca too, shouldn't I? He'll want this for the *Hog*. He can be there to document the moment I peel back the curtain like Sherlock Holmes and reveal the brilliant solution that, heretofore, even the police have failed to see."

It was at just that moment that Mrs. Malone brought in the Turkish coffee, saving Jasper from making a comment Merinda would not have appreciated.

Merinda hopped up and dashed to the blackboard. "Our suspect board."

"With which I have become very familiar over the past few months." He sipped the coffee.

"We know the obvious," Merinda said, beginning to pace. "The threatening letters that Brigid and DeLuca received were clearly sent from Gavin Crawley."

"Based on what evidence?"

"Because Gavin is left-handed, of course. The letters were clearly cut by someone who is left-handed."

Jasper shrugged. "There are hundreds of left-handed people in the city. Thousands."

"But Gavin has a *motive*, Jasper, and everything comes down to the motive. Several of the men listed on the board"—she pointed at it again, like a teacher in a classroom—"had the opportunity. But they didn't have the motive."

"And only Gavin did?"

"Precisely. Fiona's only crimes were being pretty and working for Tertius Montague. Our Mr. Crawley, as we know, has a weakness for a pretty face, as evidenced by his pursuit of Jem. Fiona must have told her new beau about an arrangement Montague had with Chief Tipton."

"Tipton?" Jasper's eyebrows rose.

"Even those in power can be bribed into silence—and to turn a blind eye to certain conditions in the city," Merinda said. "In a moment of poor judgment, Gavin Crawley opens up to Fiona about this great debt he carries. He loves living as a wealthy man, so he keeps his shoes shined and his hair plastered perfectly. But he can't resist trying his luck at the racetracks. And his fortune begins to dwindle, rapidly."

"You realize that you are overbalancing any actual detective work you have done with hefty doses of hypothesizing?" Jasper said with a grin.

"It is my *golden moment*," Merinda argued, as if that were explanation enough. "Gavin was determined to move upward, and in Fiona he saw his chance. He promised to take Fiona with him on his meteoric rise if only she kept feeding him information about Montague. Fiona, like many silly women before her, was besotted with him and the prospect he presented. Soon he learned about the involvement of your Chief Tipton. And now he had lots of puppets to play with. When Mayor Montague began talking about his new initiative to improve the morality of the city, Gavin decided it was the perfect opportunity to step closer to a man whose influence he wanted to exploit."

Jasper savored a sip of coffee. "And then?"

"You know, don't you?"

He put his cup on its saucer. "I surmised. You forget, Merinda, that I am the *actual* detective in the room. Oh, put away that scowl! You're proving more adept at this than you think."

Somewhat mollified, Merinda continued. "They quarreled

eventually. Probably Fiona began wanting more than his now-tenuous finances could give her. He wanted to be rid of her and move on to someone else, but he had told her too much." She shrugged. "So he chloroformed her. Then strangled her with a rope. We found no signs of struggle on her body because she knew him. She trusted the man who murdered her, Jasper. Can't you just see him approaching her with his dapper suit and his honey-dipped tongue?"

"Back to Fiona, please."

"Well, he paid Forbes and Tony to move the body to the theatre. Nothing would embarrass Montague more than a dead woman found in his gorgeous new theatre. And the more Gavin got in debt the more he wanted to deflect the blame. Maybe cause some confusion. Maybe paint a different villain. Fingers of accusation pointed away from Gavin, and the publicity of a dead body on that new red carpet did not please Montague. Especially as Horace Milbrook was inching ahead in the election race."

"And what about Grace?" Jasper asked, sipping from a refilled coffee cup. "Gavin again?"

"Obviously. When Fiona was killed, Grace, Fiona's friend and confidante, surmised that Gavin had done it. She confronted him and told him she knew everything. She also knew from her connections that he had bought the silence of other people in town, and she believed he would buy hers, as well. Unfortunately for her, he did want her silence, but the solution he had in mind was more permanent."

Jasper nodded approvingly. "And he has his goons drop her body at another high-profile Montague event. I must say, Merinda, you really do have a knack for this."

She stamped her foot. "Don't patronize me, Jasper. You'd figured all of this out already, hadn't you?"

"Not all of it. Your connections are ingenious. I actually didn't start piecing it together until our day at the Danforth racetrack."

Merinda nodded. "More gambling. He used Tippy for this.

Another susceptible girl easily bought." She flopped on her chair near the fireplace and threw back a glug of Turkish coffee.

"You're forgetting another woman he used," Jasper said soberly.

"Who, Jem?" Merinda shook her head. "No. Jem was never taken in by him. She knew exactly what he was. I think he was interested in her because he saw our exploits turning up in the *Hog* and he knew she worked with Tippy. But we turned the tables on him!"

There was a knock at the door, and presently Mrs. Malone came into the sitting room bearing an unsigned telegram.

Merinda's face went pale as she read.

Jasper straightened. "What?"

She crumpled the telegram and threw it at him. "Take it. Solve it. I am not solving anything anymore." She stood and faced the chalkboard. "How could I have been so stupid?"

Jasper read the telegram and sighed. "So Gavin has Jem. And Tippy. We'll find them, Merinda. We'll give him whatever he wants."

"Cracker jacks, Jasper! He was smarter than I thought. Poor Jem!" Merinda wrung her hands. "I wanted to wrap up this case, clean off the chalkboard, and move onto the next thing! Instead, the mystery I have to solve is the most important of my life. He wants to leave town and has spent the past weeks wiping Toronto clean of anything that could implicate him."

"And the last two girls who know his secrets." Jasper stared ruefully at his cup of coffee. "Where would he take two innocent females?"

"They could be anywhere in the city." She flipped through her mind's catalogue.

Jasper went to the kitchen and telephoned the station to tell them of the missing girls. He returned to the sitting room and opened his hand toward Merinda. "Time to let the police take over, Merinda. I've been happy to let you do some sleuthing on your own, but this is getting too serious. I won't let you take the risk."

"You don't *let* me do anything, Jasper Forth!" Merinda growled. "I am a free woman. Now, help me think where he might have taken them." She inhaled sharply. "The theatre! The Winter Garden! It has to be there!"

Jasper shook his head. "There's likely to be a show there on Saturday, Merinda."

"He's not remarkably intelligent," she said.

"I don't think it's the Winter Garden. Not today. That would be sloppy. Every criminal has an inherent need to put their thumbprint on whatever they do. Your M.C. Wheaton says that. Crawley won't be careless about this."

Merinda flopped backward on the settee and closed her eyes tight, torn between her desire to race about the city looking for Jem and her need to think this through logically, to understand the mind of a killer. Sherlock Holmes compared his brain to an attic, with different compartments storing necessary information. He didn't keep any information in there that would obscure the most essential facts. Merinda imagined herself in an attic looking through boxes. She went back to the box from the very beginning of their association with Gavin.

The Elgin Theatre.

The Election Gala.

The Ward.

The hidden Winter Garden Theatre.

Spenser's.

Jem falling for DeLuca, ever so slowly. Ever so obviously.

Jem looking through DeLuca's journal—

She sat up. *DeLuca's Journal.* She followed that thought for a moment, pressing the heels of her palms into her closed eyes. The man in one of the entries had had impeccable manners and a clipped voice. He'd talked about a garden and girl. A garden, a girl, and a *tunnel* Ray had thought existed only in fables.

Then she thought about the tunnel: the dampness of Fiona's clothes when they found her, the sediment under her fingernails.

She grabbed Jasper's arm so tightly she cut off its circulation. "I know where they are."

Jem thought it rather unfortunate that Gavin Crawley was holding a gun to her head. After all, she had only recently had a life-affirming moment at St. James. Tippy was there too, held tightly by Forbes. It was further unfortunate that Merinda wasn't there to fill her with confidence—or to strike these men across the head with her blasted crowbar.

She didn't know which cold, uninhabited building Gavin had brought them to, thanks to the blindfolds they'd used on her and Tippy. They'd taken Jem's off now that they were here, wherever 'here' was, and they were taking Tippy's off too. But the girl stumbled, forcing both Forbes and Gavin to reach to steady her, and it was then that Jem saw her chance.

She kicked Gavin's shin and darted off. It was only a moment before she realized that her too-high heels were slowing her down, and they made a horrid noise that was too easy to follow. She kicked them off and ran silently into the darkness.

They shouted and at least one of them gave chase, but she had the advantage for the moment. She raced down a corridor and ducked into a narrow spot beside a tall cabinet, forcing herself to breathe quietly. Forbes went through several doorways looking for her, but always he returned to the corridor where she hid. Finally he drew even with her cabinet. She held her breath.

In the end, it was a rat that ratted her out. As Forbes passed, he startled the rat from some hiding place. It dropped from a vent shaft above Jem and fell onto her head. Its horrible body and wormy tail snaked across her shoulder and its claws got tangled in her hair. And Jem could hardly be blamed for letting loose an involuntary shriek that echoed across the corridor.

"Hello there." Forbes grabbed her arm and tugged her into the half-light of the corridor. He brandished his pistol at her. "Let's get you back to—"

Jem lowered her head and bit his knuckles. It probably wasn't the pain so much as the surprise that made him drop the gun. It clattered to the floor and Jem was afraid it would go off. But it didn't, so she grabbed it and pointed it at his face. "I'm going to use it!" Jem's voice quaked. She threatened and pointed, just as she had learned from Jasper.*

"Stop that." Forbes reached out and snatched it from her. He pointed it at her nose and forced her back toward Gavin.

"Rats!" she squeaked.

⤜⤛

Where is Merinda? Jem squeezed her eyes shut. This was the second time in as many months she had been held at the whim of a man several times larger than herself while Merinda enjoyed the fresh air.†
Tippy was tied up not far from her, and Gavin was rapping his pistol on his expensive trousers. What were they planning to do with them? Jem imagined a thousand scenarios, but they all ended in death. Or at least a good deal of discomfort.

The gag cut the corners of her mouth, and her feet and hands were bound. She tried to pull free, but all she managed to do was squirm. She cursed her poor, bound frame affixed to the upturned crate.

She thought about Ray. She thought about Merinda and Jasper. Then she thought about her childhood and the letter she had just ripped up admonishing her imprudent behavior. It *was* imprudent, wasn't it? What right did she have to color so far outside the lines of propriety?

Then she thought about Tippy, and she gazed at the poor girl, tied up and as good as dead now. Jem and Merinda had put themselves

---

* After a lesson in which Merinda failed to empty the bullets out of the pistol they used for practice, Jasper declined to help any further.

† Jem recorded that first adventure in the story "A Singular and Whimsical Problem."

in danger willingly. But Tippy had approached them to *avoid* danger. And now look at her.

Gavin moved closer and traced her neckline with his finger. Jem's eyes never left the revolver at his hip level, even as he lowered his mouth, removed the bind from her lips, and brushed her with a kiss. "I've no trouble disposing of disposable women, Jemima. What I'm deciding," he said, raising the gun to her temple, "is exactly how to do it."

Chapter Twenty-One

The bank layers three levels. The lifts are to the right. Down the shaft there is a path to Victoria Street. A subterranean tunnel, built in case of siege in the City of York in the nineteenth century, begins under its foyer and snakes underneath, coming just outside Massey Hall. The tunnels are closely encased, narrow, and suffocating. So old, indeed, that no one can be sure that time and wear have not crumbled it into a dirt avalanche.

From Toronto Architecture of the New Century,
William Flanders, ed.

Merinda had changed into tweed, cotton, and suspenders and was rapping her walking stick on her palm. "I'd really rather do this alone," she said for the third time as she and Jasper sat in the cab heading toward Yonge.

Gavin Crawley had bragged in a prison cell that he knew the inner workings of Dominion Bank, so they were headed there now.

"Yes," Jasper said, also for the third time, "but then you'd actually have to *use* that ridiculous tunnel. You'd perhaps suffocate from crumbling dirt, and even if you made your way to the bank, you'd have no sure way of getting inside."

The cab deposited them at the Dominion Bank, and Jasper's identification got them past one of the two guards on duty on a Saturday.

Inside, the other guard was holding a bloody cloth to his forehead. "There's been a break in."

"I can see that," Jasper said. "I'm with the police. Your friend outside will see you get medical attention. Then both of you please call the station for backup."

The man gazed at him dizzily. "They broke in."

Jasper led Merinda across the grand foyer, their steps echoing on the tile. A few desks, sequestered with iron grates, lined each side of the bank lobby.

"The security here isn't wonderful, is it?" Merinda sniffed. "If I had an account here, I would close it."

Boom.

Jasper held Merinda back. "Hush. Someone's breaking into the safe."

Given the cavernous acoustics of the place, it was impossible to deduce whether the sound had come from above or below. Merinda only hoped it wasn't anywhere near Tippy and Jem. She still didn't know for sure that Gavin had brought them here, but the break-in at this time seemed unlikely to be coincidental.

Jasper turned to Merinda. "You go try to find Jem. I'll follow the sound and try to stop the robbery."

Merinda nodded and went out again into the grand entrance of the bank. Maybe there would be some clue there as to where Gavin had taken Jem. She'd been there less than thirty seconds when a side door opened, and she scuttled behind a pillar as a figure emerged.

Forbes.

He didn't scan the lobby at all, or he would've seen her. Instead, he concentrated on pulling the door shut behind him—it didn't want to stay latched—while he held a pistol in the other hand.

He tucked the pistol under his arm and yanked the door shut again and again, his anger growing. And Merinda seized her opportunity.

She crossed the distance quickly, silently. And when she was upon him, she dropped her walking stick and leaped onto Forbes's back.

The gun fell to the floor and he struggled to fling Merinda off, but she tightened her grip around his neck. She was strong, but he was bigger—and unpredictable. She could never calculate which way he would turn next.

He finally threw her from him. She sprawled across the floor of the lobby, very near her walking stick. She grabbed it and lunged at Forbes just as he retrieved his pistol and fired.

Merinda stopped dead in her tracks, the blood draining from her face. But she felt no pain, and now Forbes was lunging at her again.

She reared back with her crowbar and pounded him on the head with it. He collapsed in a heap.

"I should have known you'd be a wretched shot," said Merinda, and she set off through the side door in pursuit of Jem.

"I heard a gunshot!"

Jem's eyes were wide. "I did too."

Gavin swung his pistol from Jem's head and in the direction of the sound, which was down the corridor where Forbes had left them a few minutes before.

"Don't shoot!" It was Merinda's voice, echoing down the tunnel.

Gavin shook his pistol down the corridor. "Don't try anything!"

"I won't!" Merinda sounded almost chipper. "I surrender!"

That seemed to give Gavin pause, but he quickly recovered. "Get in here and sit down, then."

Merinda stepped into the room where Jem and Tippy were tied up. She was dressed in her customary trousers, of course, but she'd lost her bowler. Why had she surrendered? Jem shot her a look, but Merinda only winked.

"Where's Forbes?" Gavin asked, grabbing Merinda and beginning to tie her up.

"No idea. You brought that goon with you, did you?"

Gavin tied Merinda up, feet and hands. It annoyed Jem how cheerful Merinda seemed. Jem's own heart, by this point, was in her throat.

When Gavin had secured Merinda to his satisfaction, he waved the barrel of his pistol. "You three don't go anywhere, you hear?" He headed off down the corridor. "Forbes!"

"He's robbing the bank, Merinda!" Jem said frantically. "With Forbes."

"That much is evident, Jemima."

Jem started crying softly, a luxury she had not afforded herself before, when she'd been trying to stay strong for Tippy.

Merinda struggled against her bonds. "These ropes are pretty tight," she said.

Tippy, still gagged, silently watched Merinda, who was all smiles and sparkly eyes.

"Gavin is going to kill us," Jem said through chattering teeth. "Why are you so blasted cheerful?"

"Ooh," Merinda said, "I think my foot fell asleep."

"Merinda!" Jem said, stomping her bound feet together. "You shouldn't have come here without a plan! Do you have a plan?"

"You're not still crying, are you?"

"Yes. Yes, Merinda, I am crying. Our lives are almost over. And look at poor Tippy."

Merinda laughed. "It's not nearly as dire as all that. Jasper is here and the police are on their way. And I'll bet a dollar DeLuca's not far behind to get it all down for the *Hog*. He was the one who telegraphed that you'd been taken."

"I'm a horrible bachelor girl detective," Jem whimpered, not even brightening at the mention of Ray's name. "I wasn't cut out for this."

"Then what *were* you cut out for, Jemima?" Merinda *tsked* at her. "You're my adventurous and perfect Watson."

Jem fought back a sob. "I was cut out to tend house and have babies and marry some man who doesn't mind a girl who"—she hiccupped and gulped a few tears—"sometimes gets in danger and—"

"Nonsense, my darling Jem. Such a man does not exist."

In all of the romantic novels Jem had ever read, this would be the precise moment when the heroine would feel faint and require smelling salts. Instead, she straightened her shoulders. "I beg to differ."

"Cracker jacks," Merinda said. "You are much better off here with me."

"Better off here! With you? Perhaps the gravity of our situation is not clear to you," Jem hissed. "Gavin has a gun and he means to kill us, and our poor corpses will be found somewhere just...just like F-Fiona and Grace and..."

"Shh!" Merinda said, looking down the corridor.

Jem heard heavy footfalls. More than one set. It had to be Gavin. No one else knew they were here, did they? Oh, he would not give Jem a painless death, she knew that now. She said a quick prayer and resigned herself to whatever would come next.

But the man who stepped into the light was not Gavin, not Forbes, but Constable Jasper Forth, leading a detachment of Toronto's finest.

"Jasper!" Merinda said. "Perfect timing!"

"Merinda!" Jasper went straight to her and began working on the ropes binding her. Then he seemed to remember himself and noticed the others. "And Jem, and Tippy! What luck! Come on, gents. Hop to. Untie these ladies and let's get them out of here."

The policemen got them all untied quickly.

Jem stood, rubbing her wrists. "What happened to Gavin?"

"In custody," Jasper said, jabbing his thumb in the direction of the corridor. "Forbes too. Waiting for the paddywagon."

"Good," Jem said, and promptly fainted.

Merinda adjusted her bowler and happily watched two constables trundle Forbes and Gavin out to the police automobile. A small crowd had gathered outside Dominion Bank to watch the spectacle.

Ray appeared at Merinda's shoulder.

"I suppose I should thank you," she said before he could speak. "If I hadn't read about the tunnels in your journal..."

Ray stomped on her sentence. "Wait! You read my journal too?"

"Just the interesting stuff. The Don Jail stuff. Not the boring poetry and romance stuff. You may have a knack for excavating the mire of the city in the *Hog*, DeLuca, but you really are an abysmal writer."

"And yet I saved your life." He smiled.

"I didn't know it needed saving." Merinda retorted.

"But I did!" Ray persisted. "And Jem's and Tippy's."

"How, DeLuca?"

"You know."

"Oh, your journal." Merinda shrugged. "Yes, well, perhaps you did give me a bit of a hint, mentioning the tunnel under the bank. But it was quite obvious. I would've deduced it on my own eventually."

"Ah, but in time?"

"All right, *Hogwash Herald*," Merinda said with a reluctant grin, "get out that famous journal of yours and get ready to write. Have I got a tale for you." She began extolling her brilliant plan and its brilliant execution, but she noticed that Ray was not writing anything down. "What's the matter—going too fast for you?"

"Where's Jemima?" Ray asked.

"Jasper's taking Jem to the hospital."

"*What?*"

"Would you look at that?"

"What?"

"Your face, DeLuca. And she thinks *she's* the obvious one. They're stitching her head up. Just a little bump from her heroic detective work. She'll be home in time for tea."

"I...I...that's wonderful to hear."

Merinda clutched his arm. "Now, about that front page headline..."

Jem woke up in motion. She found herself on a stretcher being loaded into what looked an awful lot like an ambulance. "What's happening?" She tried to sit up, but her head hurt, and she lay back down.

"You're going to be fine, Jem."

She blinked up at the man and tried to recall his name. "Jasper?"

Jasper's face showed relief. "Hello, Jem. You fell and hit your head. Nasty little gash there. They're taking you to the hospital for stitches."

Jem noticed red rope burns on her wrists, and she remembered she'd been tied up. She remembered it all. "Jasper, what happened? Where's Merinda?"

"Merinda's fine." Jasper kept his voice low. "One of the officers is just asking her questions. She's not hurt at all."

"Gavin Crawley!" she cried. "That cad. You got him?"

"Yes, Jem. And Forbes."

Jem let the tension flow out of her like air from a balloon. She closed her eyes and rested on the stretcher. She wouldn't think anymore. Not for a while. She wouldn't remember being scared or worried or brave and resourceful. She didn't have to be strong anymore. Someone was looking out for her, and so she let herself drift to sleep.

CHAPTER
Twenty-Two

*Every good mystery has a denouement. It pulls
back the cloak and the magic trick is revealed.
You make at last the realization your muddled
brain had previously failed to see. You can finally
reflect on all that your limited deductive powers
had missed when someone with more astute
mental faculties is there to explain in full.*

Guide to the Criminal and Commonplace, M.C. Wheaton

McCormick read over Ray's early version of the evening edition, and his face brightened. "We'll sell out of these." Something almost approaching pride flashed behind the editor's eyes.

Ray pushed his bowler back and reveled in his favorite sounds: the thrum of the machines, the feeding of the pulp and fiber into the jaws of the press. They had sold a lot of papers lately, thanks to Merinda and her golden moments. He stretched his legs out onto his desk and folded his hands behind his head. He felt a little more secure now, what with his slightly raised salary. He had even bought a new Underwood.

Ray ran his fingers through his hair, remembering the moment he had half-sleepily recognized Jem's fingers in his hair. Her breath had been so close. When he'd opened his eyes and looked up, her bright eyes had gone big and her shoulders had lurched. He remembered her sudden horror.

He'd need to map out something brilliant if he was going to sweep *that* misunderstanding under the carpet forever. She'd been humiliated and he had let her stand there humiliated. He couldn't blink away the hurt in her eyes no matter how often he tried. He got up and paced the square room, twirling his father's watch nervously around his finger.

Skip's voice stopped him mid-stride: "Mr. DeLuca, you've got a visitor."

"Skip, how many times do I have to say it? Call me Ray."

"Temper, Ray." His sister's voice came from behind Skip's shoulder. Skip ushered Viola in and took his leave with a polite nod.

"Where's Luca?" Ray wondered.

"With the neighbors." Viola looked around the office, taking in every detail. "I have never been here before. This is you? All you?"

Ray tried to see his workspace through his sister's eyes. To him, it was a few slats of crooked wood and a makeshift desk covered in papers. But Viola's eyes were misting. "I am so proud of you."

"Crying, Vi?" Ray's smile tugged at his lips.

"We are making it happen, aren't we? That life for ourselves."

Ray took her hands in his. "I would be nothing without you." He offered her a seat on a rickety chair.

Viola folded her skirt and sat. "Is this where you entertain important men for important meetings?"

Ray just laughed. "Yes. Of course. Can you imagine me having an important meeting?"

"If only Mama could see you, Ray." She folded her hands. "I'm here to tell you that you won't have to look after me and Luca anymore."

Ray blanched. "Why is that?"

"Tony has found a job in Chicago."

Ray balled his fists and tried to keep his voice even. "What kind of job?"

"Does it matter?" Viola's eyes were bright. "You can visit us there. Chicago is a much bigger city than Toronto. A city of progress. They won't mind a few more immigrants there. We can find people like us. Ray, you should come too."

Ray ran his hand over his face. "I can't."

"Of course you can." She grabbed his hand. "There are newspapers everywhere. You could probably report for the *Tribune!* Or the *Herald!* Why, you might—"

"When did you decide this?"

Viola dropped her eyes. "Tony cannot stay here. He has been...threatened, Ray. And he has found a way to make it for us over there. In America."

"Oh, Viola." Could she not see the cage closing in on her?

Her eyes were a film of tears. "Is this how it is to be? Disapproving of Tony again?"

"He was in league with murderers, Vi. There's no telling what he's done." He touched her arm. "I can support you. And Luca. Just stay here. Leave him, Vi."

She shut her eyes and exhaled. "Ray, we have talked about this."

"I don't understand Tony, and I don't understand your need to dart off to Chicago. Your family is here."

Her eyes were gentle as she looked at him. "My family is where Tony and Luca are."

"And me?"

"Ray—"

"No, Vi. I will never condone him. I will not strive to understand him. I do understand that you love him and that you think you can't help it. Even though you know..."

Despite his plea for Vi to stay, a quiet part of his brain quickly reminded him that if she and Luca were no longer his to care for, he could pursue Jem again. Could give her at least *some* of what she'd want.

But immediately a louder part of his mind recoiled at the idea. *Men like you don't marry girls like her. Men like you need to be able to take off whenever and wherever the wind leads you. Men like you cannot be bound to someone. Men like you—*

"Ray?"

Ray broke through his haze of thought. His anger dissipated. "I wish you would stay near me, Vi. You know I would do anything to support you and Luca."

Viola cupped Ray's chin in her palm. "Of course you would. But you will see someday, my Ray. You will see what it is to love. That sometimes the feeling binds you so tightly you forget to breathe. In those moments, you are willing to do anything. Anything to keep that feeling...to hold on to it." She opened his clenched fingers and placed her hand in his. "My Ray, I shall always think of you and pray for you. And we shall write."

"And Luca?"

"I'll take good care of him. I promise."

Ray sat there an hour after she left, feeling the humming of the machines, the force of words. Finally, he tugged his hat over his hair and set out into the night.

The Toronto sky was pinpricked by winking stars and a full moon shone over the warehouses, the church steeples, and the tall stories of the Railway Building. He reached his home on Trinity and went inside. He tossed his hat on a chair and fell back on his bed's home-spun quilt. Not a real home, of course. Just one to stay in when he wasn't pursuing a story for weeks on end.

Viola and Tony in Chicago. He squeezed his eyes tight. Chicago. What a city that would be. He couldn't control Vi's life. Until now, he had managed to be the glue that pasted the pieces of her shattered life back whenever she needed.

But now...

He looked around at the crude four walls, the sputtering stove, the sparse furniture and mismatched dishes. If Vi and Luca didn't need his care and part of his paycheck, and if he squirreled away enough of his salary, he could maybe think of moving to a larger house. One with a garden, maybe.

Jem deserved a billion beautiful gardens and a billion bright and beautiful things he could never give her. But he could give her an experience.

He'd just have to use someone else's garden.

❧

"Telegram."

Jem took it from Mrs. Malone and opened it. "I'm supposed to go to the Elgin Theatre."

"Alone?"

"Quite specifically alone." Jem showed Merinda the message.

Merinda huffed. "Why you and not me?"

Jem tossed the telegram onto the table. "Clearly, I'm your better half."

"Cracker jacks you are. I'm coming too."

Unsure of how to dress, Jem and Merinda settled on trousers and hats, shirtwaists, vests, and boots. Merinda grabbed her walking stick crowbar. If this was a new case, they would be prepared.

Both the Elgin and the Winter Garden theatres were dark on Mondays, giving the casts and crews night off. They found the lobby doors open, however, so they crept inside. They stole through the mahogany, the marble, the red. The scene of their first murder investigation.

"Aha!" Merinda spotted a note stuck to the brass railing of the stairway to the mezzanine. "Here, it's for you."

Jem learned she was to go upstairs. Alone.

"It's probably just the *Tely* wanting an inside scoop on you," sniffed Merinda.

"Here? Now? In the dark? Fiddlesticks! Just stay here," Jem said. "If I'm not down in twenty minutes, go for Jasper."

"Fine. But take this." Merinda held out her small, ivory-handled gun.

Jem slid it into her handbag. "You know I don't know how to use it."

"Threaten and point. Or smack your assailant on the head with it."

Jem strode over to the elevator. But the grate was closed and the electricity was shut down, so she had no choice but to go back out-side and around to the fire escape. The first night she had visited the Winter Garden, she'd been wearing shoes with icepick heels. This time, in boots, it was much easier to ascend all four flights of the fire escape.

She climbed through the window, and her stomach somersaulted. Empty theatres were always unnerving. But the area was well lit, as if someone had anticipated her journey upward. She stepped onto the stage.

Here she was again in the hidden fairyland. The colors met her as before—flowers everywhere, vines snaking up pillars and intertwin-ing over the ceiling, holding twigs like grasping hands, as she stepped down the stairs at the side of the stage and into the aisle.

She heard a shuffle behind her, as she'd expected to. So she kept her voice cordial: "I got your note. Who are you?"

"See, this is the problem, Jem." Her favorite voice in the world came from directly behind her.

She drew a breath sharply but didn't turn around. If it was a dream, she'd make it last as long as she could. "What is the problem?"

"The problem is that you've put yourself into a dangerous situa-tion. Again. You're here alone meeting some stranger who sent you an anonymous note!"

"I'm a detective, Ray. And *you* are no stranger. Merinda's down-stairs too. And"—her voice wobbled a bit—"I came armed. Just in case."

"You what? I'll take the gun, please."

Her fingers shook a little as she withdrew it from her bag and held it up. He reached over her shoulder for the pistol, and their fingers brushed slightly as she transferred it to him.

His breath tickled he back of her neck. Jem squeezed her eyes shut. He was so close she could feel him. Her arms yearned to reach back and grab his hands.

"Welcome to your garden, Jem. I thought you, the woman who loves the romance in everything, would appreciate the care I took."

"Now I'm the woman who loves romance? I thought I was the silly girl with a silly heart and a taste in men who are very wrong for me."

Ray rested his hand on her shoulder. "I like girls with silly hearts."

"No. Don't touch me." She shrugged him off, and when she turned to face him there were tears in her eyes. "You made me feel silly, Ray. You made me feel worthless." Every fiber and pore ached to put her arms around him, but her pride held on.

"I miss you, Jem,"

"Ha."

"You're still angry with me."

"I may be a silly girl, but I still have some dignity." She sniffed regally. "And dramatic scenes in my favorite place...they...they..." She stopped and sniffed again.

A handkerchief appeared at her shoulder, which she didn't take. "I bet your nose is cute when it's red."

"I don't like you."

"That's a shame. *Ti adoro.*"

Her breath caught. Her Italian was bad, but the air that left her lungs and the jelly that had just replaced the joints in her knees proved she could make that out, at least.

"I'm going to sit down now," he said. "In 14-G. It seems that 14-F is vacant. I apologize for the theatrical nature of this scene." He laughed at his own pun. "But I wanted to get you alone, and I wasn't about to go pounding on your front door like some sop of a suitor." He sighed deeply. "I miss your face, Jem. I trace it in my head, down to that darling smattering of freckles across your nose, every night to help me sleep. I figure if I can conjure you up as I fall asleep, then perhaps, if I am very, very lucky, I'll dream about you."

Jem stole a sideways look at him: *her* Ray, with his beautiful thoughts and terrible poetry. She went to seat 14-E, leaving a space between them, and dropped into it. She folded her hands in her lap like a lady.

"Poor choice," he said. "I hope a lady with plumes of peacock feathers in her hat sits right in front of you."

Jem snickered. "And I hope a dashing blond prince of a man with dimples comes and sits in 14-F. Tall. With blue eyes. Not with eyes the color of black licorice. Not with hair like the night sky."

"Not your type?" Ray took off his hat and ran his fingers through hair matted in the shape of the hat he had removed.

Jem's fingertips tingled, but she tightened them in her lap. "Not precisely my type, no." She flickered her eyes over his profile.

"I bet I am not as charming a companion as Gavin Crawley."

"He was awfully charming through *Figaro*. He kept leaning over and making sure I knew that the piece made a *bold statement on the human condition.*" She giggled in spite of herself.

"He only said that because he didn't understand anything that was going on. He'd probably read it somewhere and repeated it."

"But you would understand *Figaro*?"

"Of course." Then he raised both hands before him, as if making himself stop some line of thought. And when he spoke again, it was with a voice with its playful flirtation ironed out: "Jem, this is a disaster. You don't belong with someone like me."

"I don't belong with anyone, do I? A girl in trousers who follows Merinda Herringford around the city. But I need to be in your life." She settled in her seat and faced the stage in front of her. Perhaps it would be easier to say these things if she faced forward. He didn't need to see her nose wrinkle up in concentration or the lump she couldn't swallow in her throat. "I know that you'll need to chase your stories. That you don't want to be cooped up. Maybe I won't ever be the first thing in your life, but…"

He sat in silence for long seconds. "Jem," he said at last, "I'm scared."

The word rippled through her. *Scared.*

"Scared to feel back," Ray said. "I did, I always did. But I knew I wouldn't be able to keep the words from spilling out."

"*You* were scared? I was the one taking the first step! Me! I'm not even sure if I can fit the role I was meant for. To cook and clean and tend a house and raise a family and…"

"It doesn't matter to me! It never did." He smiled. "I once told you I preferred you in pants. Do you remember?"

"No." But as soon as she said it, the wheels in her mind recalled the night of the Policeman's Ball. Something about *pantaloni*. Now she smiled. "Oh."

"You're going to have to learn Italian." He patted the seat between them. "14-F looks rather lonely. Where do you suppose your prince is?"

"If we take much longer, Merinda will occupy it."

Ray moved to 14-F. They were shoulder to shoulder, face to face. He inched closer and their noses just touched.

"Hello," Jem whispered.

"You're awfully, awfully beautiful. *Sei molto bella.*"

Jem wasn't sure she needed to learn Italian. If he kept saying *those* things in *that* voice, she doubted she'd need a translation.

The funny thing about happily-ever-after moments, Jem thought, is that they never aligned with what one's mind had concocted in years of dream-weaving. But then the heart catches up with the head, urges one to hold on, slow down, and make it last as long as possible.

Ray kissed her. He kissed away her white picket fences and matching dishes. He kissed away the cello music she had selected for the wedding ceremony. All she wanted was to be near him and hear every thought that entered his head before he even had time to scrawl it into his journal, even before he had the opportunity to filter it into English.

"You have to open your lips," he said, delightfully frustrated. "I can't work with this."

She squeaked. "How am I already bad at this?"

"It's still a big improvement from last time," he said, his breathing uneven on her cheek. "And you're just learning."

"You're going to teach me?"

He let his eyes brush over her face as if painting a picture. "Something like that."

"I wore you down," she said triumphantly as she paused to catch her breath.

"To absolutely nothing."

"But it was worth it, wouldn't you say?"

He wasn't sure. But change coursed through him, starting to take the stubbornness and fear in stride, replacing both with a conviction that obliterated the differences between them. He knew he was being selfish, even as his mind thought ahead to the million ways he would try to change the world for her. And he knew she deserved better. "Yes it was worth it," he finally said before leaning in for another kiss.

She opened her lips under his for just a moment, but then she pulled back, her eyes bright as she looked at him. "I suppose you know what this means."

"What does this mean?" he asked cautiously.

"The first man I kiss is the man I will marry, remember?" She cocked her eyebrow, and a slight flush colored her cheeks. "And I've kissed you twice."

Ray tried to swallow the clammy feeling in his throat. "The first one doesn't count," he said slowly.

"But this one does."

"Jemima Watts." He stared into her face, which was all starlight and expectation. "Are you asking a man to marry you?"

"Yes," she said brazenly. "I am asking *you* to marry me."

"Then yes," he said before he could run it through his mind or even blink. He patted his pocket. "I don't have a ring."

"I suppose it isn't customary when the woman proposes to you."

He pulled out his father's watch. The only possession that mattered to him. He pressed it into her hand. Like a token or a promise. A past and a future, all ticking along underneath battered bronze and worn edges and rusty chain.

Then he turned her so she could see the whole of the theatre in flowers, painted pastorals, and pastels. "I told you your first real kiss should be in a garden."

EPILOGUE

Merinda Herringford turned from side to side in front of the mirror, admiring her new bobbed curls. All the girls in Paris were wearing it this way, she had read. It was the Bohemian style. She rocked back and forth on her heels, then plopped on the settee. Cracker jacks, the house was quiet. She and Jem had settled so nicely into the clockwork of their lives, and now the woman had the misfortune to be getting married! Merinda could just as easily think of separating from Jem as she could of sawing off her right hand.

She turned to the empty chair in the sitting room and said again what she'd said when Jem had last sat in it. "We haven't finished yet, Jem! We jumped one hurdle. But the Morality Squad is as insufferable as ever, and as long as Tertius Monague is in office, women and immigrants will be exploited the city over."

Merinda paused, and in her mind she could see and hear Jem's reply. "We never anticipated we could fix it with one sweeping gesture. It will take more than just us."

"You'll be too distracted," Merinda had whined. "You'll be consumed with laundry and that man and babies!" It couldn't be over...it simply couldn't be.

"Cabbagetown isn't the other side of the world," Jem had assured her.

But Merinda felt—then and now—that it was indeed a world away. "Someday," she told the empty chair, "we will be back in the game."

Mrs. Malone stood in the doorway. "I hesitate to interrupt your...conversation," she said, "but Jasper Forth is here."

Merinda flounced her curls. "Very well. Show him in."

Jasper came into the parlor and Mrs. Malone went for tea and scones.

"My purgatory has ended!" Jasper was happy.

"Whatever do you mean?" Merinda said, sitting and indicating that he should do the same.

Jasper wore a broad-striped casual jacket, checkered trousers, and two-toned shoes. He sat on the sofa and put his hat in his lap. "As of Monday, I can return to my post."

"Detective Constable Jasper Forth once more!" she said. "Congratulations!"

"Thank you."

"And now you will be Toronto's most effective detective, of course, seeing as you are backed by the deductive prowess of Herringford and Watts."

"Don't you mean Herringford and *DeLuca*?" Jasper asked pointedly.

"Herringford and Watts. I've already had the signs made. Besides, our clientele expects the same names they see in the *Hog*."

He scoffed again. "And how will that play out, Merinda? You're going to rouse Jem at all hours—a respectable married woman—to trail after you in trousers?"

"Respectable married woman?" Merinda laughed. "Listen to you."

"Life will change, Merinda. You don't want to be left behind."

She ignored him, opting for a different thread of conversation. "I really ought to thank you," she said.

"To thank me?" Jasper repeated, astonished.

"Yes," she said, her eyes on her hands. "I know it would have been easy for you to take what we learned at the Danforth racetrack and try and get your job back. But you maintained our confidentiality, and that allowed Herringford and Watts to solve our first major crime."

Jasper cleared his throat. "Yes, well. There are more important things than mysteries." He reached into his coat pocket and extracted an envelope. "But I didn't come here to be thanked. I found something that might be of interest to you."

He handed over the envelope, and Merinda removed and unfolded a slip of paper: *No great idea in its beginning can ever be within the law. How can it be within the law? The law is stationary. The law is fixed. The law is a chain that binds us all.*

"Interesting," she said. "Though odd, coming from an officer of the law."

"It's a quotation from Emma Goldman. The radical anarchist."

"Emma Goldman," Merinda repeated, looking even more interested.

"She'll be in Toronto next month. She's been causing quite a stir in the States. Keeps getting arrested, locked up, and tossed over here where she's safe. She was here several years ago, raising money for some society of hers."

"And you thought I'd be likely to go hear her speak?" Merinda asked.

"Emma Goldman never appears anywhere without both bringing and summoning a corps of anarchists." He looked at her appreciatively. "Merinda Herringford, I predict we are soon to have a bit of a revolution on our hands."

Merinda clapped. "Do you really think so, Jasper? Do you really?"

"I don't think you should be so happy about it."

"Cracker jacks!" Merinda said merrily. "A radical revolution! Imagine." She stretched her legs in front of the fire and crossed them at the ankles. "Demonstrations in the streets. The city on fire!" She threw a glance in the direction of the circled names on her blackboard, her mind churning with ideas for reform. "As I told you, Jasper, the adventure is only just beginning."

"It is?"

Merinda sprang from her chair, took his face in her hands, and kissed him hard on the cheek.

Jasper sputtered and blinked and then leaned toward her hopefully. She was so excited she kissed his other cheek. "It is, Jasper! It *is!*"

Dear Jemima,

Your mother and I learned recently of your marriage to an immigrant Papist.

If we hadn't already cut you off completely, we would be doing so now.

We can merely speculate what we possibly did to inspire such wayward behavior in our only daughter.

We will pray for you and hope that you spare us a thought now and then.

In their new semi-detached house in Cabbagetown, Jem kept the telegram near. During the daylight she kept it in her pocket. At night, it was in her memory as she squeezed her eyes shut in the starlight-spattered room.

One night, as moonlight latticed the curtains she had sewn and hung in their small bedroom, she heard a persistent tapping and jolted awake.

She didn't notice that Ray, too, was awake: black eyes staring above him, mind obsessed with a slight crack in the ceiling.

While Ray feigned sleep, Jem folded her legs over the side of the bed, crept to the window, and through the curtain made out a figure under the starlight.

It was Merinda, of course, waving hard and fast for her to hurry up.

Jem tiptoed to the wardrobe and pulled out trousers and a cotton shirt that she slid over her nightgown, its folds soon tucked in and safely constricted by a belt she pulled tight. She stepped into her scuffed, rubber-soled shoes. She twisted her hair into a braid, wondering how she would hide it now that she didn't have the costume trunk and its variety of headgear. Then she remembered she didn't need it—she had something better.

She slipped quietly to the mismatched table adjacent her bed where a worn old bowler sat with a frayed rim. Ray wouldn't miss it before tomorrow.

She didn't see his eyes flutter open to watch her shadow tiptoe out. Nor did she hear him when he rose a moment later to shut the door behind her.

"A missing pocket-watch," Ray heard through the slightly ajar window. Merinda was explaining the specifics of the case.

"A pocket watch!" Jem laughed. "You woke me up for a pocket watch?"

And then they set off into the night.

Toronto was cloaked in stillness. An owl hooted and a raccoon's fleeting footfall skittered across their path. A blonde girl in a bowler hat leaned into her companion and spun an excited tale of radical revolutionaries and a city that was their own, even as they wound its dark street.

Author's Note

There are no factual figures in *The Bachelor Girl's Guide to Murder*—even M.C. Wheaton and Dorothea Fairfax are figments of my imagination—and I took several historical liberties in creating Jem and Merinda's world.

While the *Globe and Mail* and the *Tely* were daily papers in Toronto, the only accurate thing about their representation here are their names. The *Hogtown Herald* is a complete fiction.

The King Edward Hotel and St. James Cathedral are just some of the real places I used, though their owners and the events therein are completely fictional. Perhaps the most imaginative liberty was taken with the Elgin and Winter Garden Theatres, which didn't open until 1913 and whose proprietor, Frederick Loewe, was absolutely not a criminal. If you ever have the opportunity to visit, you will see why I wanted to make it a part of my fictional landscape.

My favorite historical fiction inspires my interest in a period and setting through capturing an essence of the long-ago world. Thus, I did try to capture the essence that was the transient city of Toronto in the early 1900s. It saw a remarkable wave of immigrants crossing over the Bridge of Sighs, many scraping by in St. John's Ward and many the victims of poor working conditions, flophouses, and unfair wages.

The Morality Squad is also a figment of my imagination, although women's courts and arrests for female incorrigibility are a sadly true part of Toronto's history. The Ontario Female Refuge's Act of 1897 made sure that anyone at all could charge a woman aged sixteen to thirty-five with charges of idleness, dissolution, and incorrigibility. Prison stints and incarceration at the notorious Mercer Reformatory in Toronto were believed to be the cure for everything from pick-pocketing to familial estrangement and suspected immorality.

Social reform and political change were very much hot topics—as they continue to be today. Toronto remains one of the most multi-cultural cities in the world.

The book *Toronto's Girl Problem: The Perils and Pleasures of the City,* by Carolyn Strange, sheds some light on the prejudice awaiting single working women moving to the city in the Edwardian age. *Bachelor Girl,* by Besty Israel, provided an interesting look at the history of unmarried women throughout history. If you would like to learn more about some of the books and websites I consulted (and take a glimpse at some of the many wonderful photographs preserved from Edwardian Toronto), please visit my website at www.rkmcmillan. com. The Toronto Reference Library, with their amazing archives and materials (and their attached Balzac's coffee location), were influential in the creation of this world.

ABOUT THE AUTHOR

Rachel McMillan is a keen history enthusiast and a lifelong bibliophile. When not writing or reading, she can most often be found drinking tea and watching British miniseries. Rachel lives in bustling Toronto, where she works in educational publishing and pursues her passion for art, literature, music, and theater.

Other Books by Rachel McMillan

A Singular and Whimsical Problem

Christmas, 1910. Merinda Herringford and Jem Watts would be enjoying the season a lot more if they weren't forced to do their own laundry and cooking. Just as they are adapting to their trusty housekeeper's ill-timed vacation, they are confronted by the strangest mystery they've encountered since they started their private investigation firm.

In this bonus e-only novella, what begins as the search for a missing cat leads to a rabble-rousing suffragette and the disappearance of several young women from St. Jerome's Reformatory for Incorrigible Females. From the women's courts of City Hall to Toronto's seedy docks and into the cold heart of the underground shipping industry, this will be the most exciting Christmas the girls have had yet...if they can stay alive long enough to enjoy it.

A Lesson in Love and Murder

The legacy of literary icon Sherlock Holmes is alive and well in 1912 Canada, where best friends Merinda Herringford and Jem Watts continue to develop their skills as consulting detectives.

The city of Toronto has been thrown into upheaval by the arrival of radical anarchist Emma Goldman. Amid this political chaos, Benny Citrone of the Royal North-West Mounted Police arrives at Merinda and Jem's flat, requesting assistance in locating his runaway cousin—a man with a deadly talent.

While Merinda eagerly accepts the case, she finds herself constantly butting heads—and hearts—with Benny. Meanwhile, Jem has her own hands full with a husband who is distracted by his sister's problems but still determined to keep Jem out of harm's way.

As Merinda and Jem close in on the danger they've tracked from Toronto to Chicago, will they also be able to resolve the troubles threatening their future happiness before it's too late?

Independence, love, and lives are at stake in *A Lesson in Love and Murder*, the gripping second installment of the Herringford and Watts Mysteries series.